Our Town
A Play in Three Acts

by
Thornton Wilder

A SAMUEL FRENCH ACTING EDITION

SAMUEL FRENCH
FOUNDED 1830

SAMUELFRENCH.COM

**IMPORTANT BILLING AND CREDIT
REQUIREMENTS**

All producers of *OUR TOWN must* give credit to the Author of the Play in all programs distributed in connection with performances of the Play, and in all instances in which the title of the Play appears for the purposes of advertising, publicizing or otherwise exploiting the Play and/or a production. The name of the Author *must* appear on a separate line on which no other name appears, immediately following the title and *must* appear in size of type not less than fifty percent of the size of the title type.

This play may be performed only in its entirety. No permission can be granted for cuttings, readings or any use of single acts or parts of the play for any purpose whatsoever without the express written permission of the Wilder Family LLC. Absolutely *no* changes can be made to the text.

Additional production materials available:

Artwork Logo Packs
Sound Effects CD

The above items are available to licensed groups only. Please visit **www.samuelfrench.com** for specific prices and ordering information.

FOREWORD TO *OUR TOWN*

You hold in your hands the *definitive* acting edition of Thornton Wilder's American classic *Our Town*, in short, the words of the play as the author wanted them spoken on the stage.

A Brief History of *Our Town* in Print

Our Town had its world premiere on Broadway at Henry Miller's Theatre on February 4, 1938. That same year, Coward-McCann published a trade edition of the play that Wilder had submitted before rehearsals began in December of 1937. The first Samuel French acting edition, which enshrined the Broadway production stage manager's prompt copy of the play, appeared in print in 1939. But it wasn't until 1956, nearly two decades later, that Thornton Wilder, drawing on these two texts, as well as his extensive involvement with the play in a variety of ways including production, translations, adaptations – even as an actor – finally sat down to craft his definitive version of *Our Town*. The resulting text contained over 700 changes, most of which involved stage directions and punctuation. Wilder asked that this version be used in all subsequent reprints of both the reading and acting editions of the play.

The new reading edition of Wilder's *Our Town* appeared in print for the first time in October of 1957 when Harper & Bros. (now HarperCollins) published *Three Plays*, a trade publication containing the definitive editions of *Our Town, The Skin of Our Teeth,* and *The Matchmaker.* (This volume, still in print today, includes a preface by Wilder in which he famously describes *Our Town* as "an attempt to find a value above all price for the smallest events in our daily life.") Three years later, in 1960, Harper & Bros also published its own single-play edition, which formally replaced the earlier 1938 trade edition. But for reasons that have never been clear, the Samuel French acting edition was never updated to reflect Wilder's 1957 definitive take on his play – until now.

So it is that Samuel French and the Wilder family find themselves in the happy position, as part of the celebration of the 75th Anniversary of the play's opening on the Great White Way, of presenting to the theatrical community the definitive acting edition of *Our Town*. For the first time in history, all existing published versions of the play share the same text.

This acting edition is still the *Our Town* that we have been familiar with for decades. It has been available in bookstores and libraries since 1957. Since then, professional theatres have been encouraged – and in recent years have been required – to use this version of the text for their productions of *Our Town*. For the most part, the differences between the two acting editions involve changes in stage directions and punctuation. While subtle, they represent an important shift in tone, making the play more understated, less sentimental, and ultimately more universal.

From Reading Edition to Acting Edition

Transforming Wilder's definitive 1957 reading edition of *Our Town* into this acting edition required a shift in format from a book designed to serve the needs of the individual reader to a manual for staging a production.

To insure that the new acting edition would reflect all of Wilder's final adjustments in dialogue and punctuation, we used Wilder's 1957 definitive edition as a basis. Once the script was formatted, we carefully reviewed the blocking and stage directions. Part of this process involved repositioning some of the directions included in the 1957 text that had been grouped to enhance a reading experience. These stage directions have not been changed; rather, their placement has been adjusted for the benefit of actors and directors so that the blocking anticipates the lines of dialogue to which it relates. We also restored some of the detailed stage directions that were not appropriate for earlier reading editions of the play. Examples of such notes include lighting and sound effect cues and the detailed pantomime performed by Mrs. Gibbs and Mrs. Webb in their kitchens. With the exception of overly precise and confusing directions ("Xing two steps L. of L.C.") or blocking that contradicts the shift in the emotional tenor that Wilder indicated in his definitive treatment, (the instructions requiring Emily to weep throughout the scene in Mr. Morgan's drugstore in Act II), all blocking from the original acting edition has been restored in the construction of this new acting edition.

Finally, we reviewed the supplementary material in the 1939 acting edition: including the costume, property, scenic design, doubling and understudy plots, and Wilder's own notes to directors. (By the 1950s, the acting edition's original unwieldy thirteen-page lighting plot had been dropped from the text.) Our goal here was self-evident: to preserve the historical record of the play. And this we have done happily, with two exceptions: we have dropped from this new edition the simplistic synopsis called the "Story of the Play" and the listing of outdated press quotes intended to help companies publicize the show. In order to assist theatres producing *Our Town*, we have also taken this opportunity to add new supplementary material: the music and lyrics for "Blest Be The Ties That Bind" and "Art Thou Weary, Art Thou Languid."

In 1938, Wilder spoke of *Our Town* as "the life of a village against the life of the stars." Wherever it is performed, may this famous work continue to give much pleasure to all those who produce it, act in it, and encounter it on the other side of the non-curtain. It is indeed significant that in this new century Thornton Wilder's *Our Town* – whether it be presented in a city or a town, indoors or under the stars, will henceforth be performed as the playwright intended it to be performed.

***

Many hands and eyes have contributed to this project, and long hours have gone into it. It is an honor for me to conclude this note by thanking the devoted staff at Samuel French, with whom it has been a privilege to work. Rosey Strub has carried the heavy water on the Wilder side. The Wilder family thanks her and takes special pleasure in knowing that her name now has an on-going presence in this publication.

Tappan Wilder
October, 2012

SOME SUGGESTIONS FOR THE DIRECTOR

It is important to maintain a continual *dryness* of tone – the New England understatement of sentiment, of surprise, of tragedy. A shyness about emotion. These significances are conveyed by the eyes and a sharpening and distinctness of the voice. (So in the Stage Manager on the Civil War veterans: "All they knew was the name, friends – the United States of America. The United States of America." And in all the dealings of the mothers with their children where a matter-of-factness overlays the concern.)

It has already been proven that absence of scenery does not constitute a difficulty and that the cooperative imagination of the audience is stimulated by that absence. There remain, however, two ways of producing the play. One, with a constant subtle adjustment of lights and sound effects; and one through a still bolder acknowledgment of artifice and make-believe: the rooster's crow, the train and factory whistles, and school bells frankly, man-made and in the spirit of "play". I am inclined to think that this latter approach, though apparently "amateurish" and rough at first, will prove the more stimulating in the end and will prepare for the large claim on attention and imagination in the last act. The scorn of verisimilitude throws all the greater emphasis on the ideas which the play hopes to offer.

It seems advisable that at the opening of the play where the audience is first introduced to pantomime and imaginary props, that Mrs. Gibbs and Mrs. Webb in the preparation of breakfast perform much of their business with their backs to the audience, and do not distract and provoke its attention with too distinct and perhaps puzzling a picture of the many operations of coffee-grinding, porridge-stirring, etc.

At the beginning of the wedding scene there is an abrupt change of approach. The audience is hearing the thoughts of the characters and is seeing a symbolical statement of attitudes that never were consciously expressed by the characters in their daily life. This change is greatly aided by the entrance of the bride and groom through the aisles of the auditorium; and by the fact that it is accompanied by the very soft singing of the hymns by the congregation. It would be well that George on arriving on the stage draws back well toward the proscenium, indicating that this scene does not literally take place in the church or before the church. After Mrs. Gibbs's line: "George! If anyone should hear you! Now stop. Why, I'm ashamed of you!" George passes his hand over his forehead, as though emerging from a dream, and with a complete change of matter, returning to realism, explains: "What? Where's Emily?" Mrs. Gibbs and George do not touch each other during the scene until she straightens his tie, and the strong emotion is indicated by tension, not by weeping. In the following scene between Emily and her father, however, Emily is in tears and flings herself into her father's arms.

The Stage Manager/Clergyman's speech: "I've married over two hundred couples in my day," etc., is not delivered to the village congregation before him, but across their heads, an almost dreamy meditation, during which the tableau on the stage "freezes".

In the last act it is important to remove from the picture of the seated dead any suggestion of the morbid or lugubrious. They sit easily; there is nothing of the fixed and unwinking about their eyes. The impression is of patient composed waiting.

Emily's revisiting her home and her farewell to the world is under strong emotion, but the emotion is that of wonder rather than of sadness. Even the "I love you all, everything!" is realization and discovery as much as it is poignancy.

Thornton Wilder
April, 1939

OUR TOWN was first performed at the McCarter Theatre, Princeton, New Jersey, on January 22, 1938.

The first New York performance of *OUR TOWN* was at Henry Miller's Theatre, February 4, 1938. It was produced and directed by Jed Harris. The technical director was Raymond Sovey; the costumes were designed by Madame Hélène Pons. The cast was as follows:

STAGE MANAGER.................................. Frank Craven

DR. GIBBS... Jay Fassett

JOE CROWELL .... Raymond Roe

HOWIE NEWSOME................................. Tom Fadden

MRS. GIBBS....................................... Evelyn Varden

MRS. WEBB .... Helen Carew

GEORGE GIBBS .... John Craven

REBECCA GIBBS................................... Marilyn Erskine

WALLY WEBB .... Charles Wiley, Jr.

EMILY WEBB....................................... Martha Scott

PROFESSOR WILLARD............................. Arthur Allen

MR. WEBB .... Thomas W. Ross

WOMAN IN THE BALCONY .... Carrie Weller

MAN IN THE AUDITORIUM......................... Walter O. Hill

LADY IN THE BOX .... Aline McDermott

SIMON STIMSON .... Philip Coolidge

MRS. SOAMES..................................... Doro Merande

CONSTABLE WARREN .... E. Irving Locke

SI CROWELL....................................... Billy Redfield

BASEBALL PLAYERS .... Alfred Ryder, William Roehrick, Thomas Coley

SAM CRAIG.. Francis G. Cleveland

JOE STODDARD .... William Wadsworth

ASSISTANT STAGE MANAGERS .... Thomas Morgan, Alfred Ryder

PEOPLE OF THE TOWN.............. Carrie Weller, Alice Donaldson, Walter O. Hill, Arthur Allen, Charles Melody, Katharine Raht, Mary Elizabeth Forbes, Dorothy Nolan, Jean Platt, Barbara Brown, Alida Stanley, Barbara Burton, Lyn Swann, Dorothy Ryan, Shirley Osborn, Emily Boileau, Ann Weston, Leon Rose, John Irving Finn, Van Shem, Charles Walters, William Short, Frank Howell, Max Beck, James Malaidy, Charles Wiley, Sr.

CHARACTERS

(in the order of their appearance)

STAGE MANAGER
DR. GIBBS
JOE CROWELL
HOWIE NEWSOME
MRS. GIBBS
MRS. WEBB
GEORGE GIBBS
REBECCA GIBBS
WALLY WEBB
EMILY WEBB
PROFESSOR WILLARD
MR. WEBB
WOMAN IN THE BALCONY
MAN IN THE AUDITORIUM
LADY IN THE BOX
SIMON STIMSON
MRS. SOAMES
CONSTABLE WARREN
SI CROWELL
THREE BASEBALL PLAYERS
SAM CRAIG
JOE STODDARD
FARMER MCCARTY
MAN AMONG THE DEAD
WOMAN AMONG THE DEAD

SETTING

The entire play takes place in Grover's Corners, New Hampshire.

THE DOUBLING AND UNDERSTUDY PLOT

1) **PROFESSOR WILLARD**: sings in choir, plays **A MAN AMONG THE DEAD**, understudies **STAGE MANAGER** and **MR. WEBB**.

2) **WOMAN IN BALCONY**: sings in choir, plays **A WOMAN AMONG THE DEAD**, understudies **MRS. WEBB, MRS. SOAMES**.

3) **MAN IN AUDITORIUM**: plays **BASEBALL PLAYER**, is **ASSISTANT STAGE MANAGER**, understudies **GEORGE**.

4) **LADY IN THE BOX**: sings in choir, understudies **MRS. GIBBS**.

5) **BASEBALL PLAYER**: is **ASSISTANT STAGE MANAGER**, understudies **SIMON STIMSON** and **SAM CRAIG**.

6) **FARMER MCCARTY**: understudies **CONSTABLE WARREN, JOE STODDARD**, and **A MAN AMONG THE DEAD**.

7) **STAGE MANAGER**: plays **SAM CRAIG**, understudies **HOWIE NEWSOME** and **PROFESSOR WILLARD**.

8) **CHOIR SINGER**: understudies **DOC GIBBS**, and **MAN IN AUDITORIUM**.

9) **CHOIR SINGER**: understudies **EMILY** and **REBECCA**, and **LADY IN BOX**, and **WOMAN IN BALCONY**.

If no understudy is engaged for the **THREE BOYS**:

> In case of illness of **JOE CROWELL**, scene must be cut and **STAGE MANAGER**'s succeeding speech also cut.

> **WALLY** understudies **SI CROWELL** (**STAGE MANAGER**'s introductory line being changed accordingly to cover **WALLY**).

> **SI. CROWELL** understudies **WALLY** (with same change in Act II)

BASEBALL PLAYERS can be reduced from three to two without changes in lines.

Lines of **A WOMAN FROM AMONG THE DEAD** can be spoken by **MRS. SOAMES**.

Lines of **A MAN FROM AMONG THE DEAD** can be spoken by **FARMER MCCARTY**.

ACT I

(no curtain)

(no scenery)

(The audience, arriving, sees an empty stage in half-light.)

(Presently the **STAGE MANAGER***, hat on and pipe in mouth, enters and begins placing a table and three chairs downstage left, and a table and three chairs downstage right.)*

(He also places a low bench at the corner of what will be the Webb house, left.)

("Left" and "right" are from the point of view of the actor facing the audience. "Up" is toward the back wall.)

(As the house lights go down he has finished setting the stage and, leaning against the right proscenium pillar, watches the late arrivals in the audience.)

(When the auditorium is in complete darkness he speaks:)

STAGE MANAGER. This play is called "Our Town". It was written by Thornton Wilder; produced and directed by A... *(or: produced by A...; directed by B...)*. In it you will see Miss C...; Miss D...; Miss E....; and Mr. F...; Mr. G...; Mr. H...; and many others. The name of the town is Grover's Corners, New Hampshire – just across the Massachusetts line: latitude 42 degrees 40 minutes; longitude 70 degrees 37 minutes.

(The lights start to glow into a dawn effect, which is followed by a gradual morning light, which increases to noon through the action of the act.)

STAGE MANAGER. *(cont.)* The First Act shows a day in our town. The day is May 7, 1901. The time is just before dawn.

(Cock crows offstage.)

The sky is beginning to show some streaks of light over in the East there, behind our mount'in. The morning star always gets wonderful bright the minute before it has to go – doesn't it?

(He stares at it for a moment, then goes upstage.)

Well, I'd better show you how our town lies. Up here – *(that is: parallel with the back wall)* – is Main Street. Way back there is the railway station; tracks go that way. Polish Town's across the tracks, and some Canuck families. *(toward the left)* Over there is the Congregational Church; across the street's the Presbyterian. Methodist and Unitarian are over there. *(off down right)* Baptist is down in the holla' by the river. Catholic Church is over beyond the tracks. Here's the Town Hall and Post Office combined; jail's in the basement. Bryan once made a speech from these very steps here. Along here's *(Main Street, parallel with the back wall)* a row of stores. Hitching posts and horse blocks in front of them. First automobile's going to come along in about five years – belonged to Banker Cartwright, our richest citizen…lives in the big white house up on the hill. Here's the grocery store and here's Mr. Morgan's drugstore. *(pointing right and left behind him)* Most everybody in town manages to look into those two stores once a day. Public School's over yonder. High School's still farther over. Quarter of nine mornings, noontimes, and three o'clock afternoons, the hull town can hear the yelling and screaming from those schoolyards. *(He approaches the table and chairs downstage right.)* This is our doctor's house, – Doc Gibbs'. This is the back door. *(Two arched trellises, covered with vines and flowers, are pushed out, one by each proscenium pillar.)*

There's some scenery for those who think they have to have scenery. This is Mrs. Gibbs' garden. Corn...peas...beans...hollyhocks...heliotrope... and a lot of burdock. *(crosses the stage)* In those days our newspaper come out twice a week – the *Grover's Corners Sentinel* – and this is Editor Webb's house. And this is Mrs. Webb's garden. Just like Mrs. Gibbs', only it's got a lot of sunflowers, too. *(He looks upward, center stage.)* Right here's... a big butternut tree. *(He returns to his place by the right proscenium pillar and looks at the audience for a minute.)* Nice town, y'know what I mean? Nobody very remarkable ever come out of it, s'far as we know. The earliest tombstones in the cemetery up there on the mountain say 1670-1680 – they're Grovers and Cartwrights and Gibbses and Herseys – same names as are around here now. Well, as I said: it's about dawn. The only lights on in town are in a cottage over by the tracks where a Polish mother's just had twins. And in the Joe Crowell house, where Joe Junior's getting up so as to deliver the paper. And in the depot, where Shorty Hawkins is gettin' ready to flag the 5:45 for Boston.

(A train whistle is heard. The **STAGE MANAGER** *takes out his watch and nods.)*

Naturally, out in the country – all around – there've been lights on for some time, what with milkin's and so on. But town people sleep late. So – another day's begun. There's Doc Gibbs comin' down Main Street now, comin' back from that baby case.

(**MRS. GIBBS**, *a plump, pleasant woman in the middle thirties, comes "downstairs" right. She pulls up an imaginary window shade in her kitchen and starts to make a fire in her stove.*)

STAGE MANAGER. *(cont.)* And here's his wife comin' downstairs to get breakfast. Doc Gibbs died in 1930. The new hospital's named after him. Mrs. Gibbs died first – long time ago, in fact. She went out to visit her daughter, Rebecca, who married an insurance man in Canton, Ohio, and died there – pneumonia – but her body was brought back here. She's up in the cemetery there now – in with a whole mess of Gibbses and Herseys – she was Julia Hersey 'fore she married Doc Gibbs in the Congregational Church over there. In our town we like to know the facts about everybody.

(**MRS. WEBB**, *a thin, serious, crisp woman, has entered her kitchen, left, tying on an apron. She goes through the motions of putting wood into a stove, lighting it, and preparing breakfast.*)

There's Mrs. Webb, coming downstairs to get her breakfast, too.

(**DR. GIBBS** *has been coming along Main Street from the left. At the point where he would turn to approach his house, he stops, sets down his – imaginary – black bag, takes off his hat, and rubs his face with fatigue, using an enormous handkerchief.*)

– That's Doc Gibbs. Got that call at half past one this morning.

(sound of newspapers sliding along the verandah)

And there comes Joe Crowell, Jr., delivering Mr. Webb's *Sentinel*.

(Suddenly, **JOE CROWELL, JR.**, *eleven, starts down Main Street from the right, hurling imaginary newspapers into doorways.)*

JOE CROWELL, JR. Morning, Doc Gibbs.

DR. GIBBS. Morning, Joe.

JOE CROWELL, JR. Somebody been sick, Doc?

DR. GIBBS. No. Just some twins born over in Polish Town.

JOE CROWELL, JR. Do you want your paper now?

DR. GIBBS. Yes, I'll take it.

*(**JOE** hands paper to **DR. GIBBS.**)*

– Anything serious goin' on in the world since Wednesday?

JOE CROWELL, JR. Yessir. My schoolteacher, Miss Foster, 's getting married to a fella over in Concord.

DR. GIBBS. I declare. – How do you boys feel about that?

JOE CROWELL, JR. Well, of course, it's none of my business – but I think if a person starts out to be a teacher, she ought to stay one. *(starts off, throwing papers)*

*(**MRS. GIBBS** crosses to stove to put bacon in skillet.)*

DR. GIBBS. How's your knee, Joe?

JOE CROWELL, JR. *(stops)* Fine, Doc, I never think about it at all. Only like you said, it always tells me when it's going to rain. *(starts off again, throwing papers)*

DR. GIBBS. What's it telling you today? Goin' to rain?

JOE CROWELL, JR. No, sir.

DR. GIBBS. Sure?

*(**MRS. WEBB** puts coffee on stove.)*

JOE CROWELL, JR. Yessir.

DR. GIBBS. Knee ever make a mistake?

JOE CROWELL, JR. No, sir.

(JOE goes off. DR. GIBBS stands reading his paper. MRS. GIBBS crosses to cupboard, cuts several slices of bread, then cuts a pie.)

(MRS. WEBB mixes, rolls, and cuts biscuits at table by stove.)

STAGE MANAGER. Want to tell you something about that boy Joe Crowell there. Joe was awful bright – graduated from high school here, head of his class. So he got a scholarship to Massachusetts Tech. Graduated head of his class there, too. It was all wrote up in the Boston paper at the time.

(DR. GIBBS turns paper inside out, yawns. MRS. GIBBS opens cupboard for tablecloth, crosses to spread it on table, crosses to cupboard for cup and spoon, crosses to set them on table for DR. GIBBS.)

Goin' to be a great engineer, Joe was. But the war broke out and he died in France. – All that education for nothing.

(The sound of milkbottles is heard offstage.)

HOWIE NEWSOME. *(off left)* Giddap, Bessie! What's the matter with you today?

(MRS. GIBBS crosses to stove, turns bacon, breaks four eggs into skillet.)

STAGE MANAGER. Here comes Howie Newsome, deliverin' the milk.

(HOWIE NEWSOME, about thirty, in overalls, comes along Main Street from the left, walking beside an invisible horse and wagon and carrying an imaginary rack with milk bottles. The sound of clinking milk bottles. The sound of clinking milk bottles continues through HOWIE's scene except when he sets down the rack. He stops center to talk to DR. GIBBS.)

HOWIE NEWSOME. Morning, Doc.

DR. GIBBS. Morning, Howie.

HOWIE NEWSOME. Somebody sick?

DR. GIBBS. Pair of twins over to Mrs. Goruslawski's.

HOWIE NEWSOME. *(starting towards Mrs. Webb's trellis)* Twins, eh? This town's gettin' bigger every year.

DR. GIBBS. Goin' to rain, Howie?

HOWIE NEWSOME. No, no. Fine day – that'll burn through.

(horse whinny off left)

Come on, Bessie. *(sets rack down, sets out two bottles in trellis)*

DR. GIBBS. Hello Bessie.

(He strokes the horse, which has remained center.)

How old is she, Howie?

HOWIE NEWSOME. *(takes rack, crosses towards* **MRS. GIBBS***)* Going on seventeen. Bessie's all mixed up about the route ever since the Lockharts stopped takin' their quart of milk every day.

*(***MRS. GIBBS***, after glancing at* **HOWIE** *through window, crosses to trellis.)*

HOWIE NEWSOME. She wants to leave 'em a quart just the same – keeps scolding me the hull trip.

(He reaches **MRS. GIBBS** *' back door. She is waiting for him.)*

MRS. GIBBS. *(opening the door, which she leaves open)* Good morning, Howie.

HOWIE NEWSOME. *(sets rack down and hands her two bottles)* Morning, Mrs. Gibbs. Doc's just comin' down the street.

MRS. GIBBS. Is he? Seems like you're late today.

HOWIE NEWSOME. Yes. Somep'n went wrong with the separator. Don't know what 'twas.

(He passes **DR. GIBBS** *up center on his way offstage.)*

Doc!

DR. GIBBS. Howie!

MRS. GIBBS. *(taking milk to cupboard and calling upstairs)* Children! Children! Time to get up.

HOWIE NEWSOME. Come on, Bessie!

(He goes off right.)

MRS. GIBBS. George! Rebecca!

*(**MRS. WEBB** puts biscuits in oven, gets tablecloth, dishes, etc., from cupboard and lays table, making several trips.)*

*(**DR. GIBBS** arrives at his back door and passes through the trellis into his house.)*

MRS. GIBBS. *(taking bread from the cupboard to the table)* Everything all right, Frank?

DR. GIBBS. Yes. I declare – easy as kittens.

MRS. GIBBS. *(crossing to stove for coffee pot)* Bacon'll be ready in a minute. Set down and drink your coffee. *(crossing to pour coffee in his cup, then sets pot back on stove)* You can catch a couple hours' sleep this morning, can't you?

DR. GIBBS. *(crossing to the sink and washing his hands)* Hm!...Mrs. Wentworth's coming at eleven. Guess I know what it's about, too. Her stummick ain't what it ought to be.

MRS. GIBBS. *(picks silverware out of a drawer)* All told, you won't get more'n three hours' sleep. Frank Gibbs, I don't know what's goin' to become of you. I do wish I could get you to go away someplace and take a rest. I think it would do you good.

MRS. WEBB. Emileeee! Time to get up! Wally! Seven o'clock!

MRS. GIBBS. *(crossing to set three places at the table)* I declare, you got to speak to George. Seems like something's come over him lately. He's no help to me at all. I can't even get him to cut me some wood.

DR. GIBBS. (*Drying his hands at the sink.* **MRS. GIBBS** *is busy at the stove.*) Is he sassy to you?

MRS. GIBBS. No. He just whines! All he thinks about is that baseball – George! Rebecca! You'll be late for school.

DR. GIBBS. M-m-m...

MRS. GIBBS. George!

DR. GIBBS. George, look sharp!

GEORGE'S VOICE. Yes, Pa!

(*MRS. GIBBS turns eggs.*)

DR. GIBBS. (*as he goes off the stage*) Don't you hear your mother calling you? I guess I'll go upstairs and get forty winks.

(*He exits upstairs.*)

MRS. WEBB. Walleee! Emileee! You'll be late for school! Walleee! You wash yourself good or I'll come up and do it myself. (*serves two dishes of oatmeal, which she places on the table*)

REBECCA. (*offstage*) Ma! What dress shall I wear?

MRS. GIBBS. (*crosses to cupboard for two plates and crosses to stove*) Don't make a noise. Your father's been out all night and needs his sleep. I washed and ironed the blue gingham for you special. (*serves one plate and sets it on the table for* **GEORGE**)

REBECCA. Ma, I hate that dress.

MRS. GIBBS. Oh, hush-up-with-you.

REBECCA. Every day I go to school dressed like a sick turkey.

MRS. GIBBS. (*serves second plate*) Now, Rebecca, you always look *very* nice.

REBECCA. Mama, George's throwing soap at me.

MRS. GIBBS. (*crossing to set plate for* **REBECCA**) I'll come and slap the both of you, – that's what I'll do.

(*A factory whistle sounds.*)

STAGE MANAGER. We've got a factory in our town, too – hear it? Makes blankets. Cartwrights own it and it brung 'em a fortune.

(The **CHILDREN** *dash in and take their places at the tables. Right,* **GEORGE,** *about sixteen, and* **REBECCA,** *eleven. Left,* **EMILY** *and* **WALLY,** *same ages. They carry strapped school-books.)*

*(***MRS. GIBBS** *crosses to stove for coffee pot, pours coffee for* **GEORGE,** *replaces pot on stove, crosses to cupboard to pour glass of milk, places it on the table for* **REBECCA,** *goes to cupboard for butter.)*

MRS. WEBB. Children! Now I won't have it. Breakfast is just as good as any other meal and I won't have you gobbling like wolves. It'll stunt your growth, – that's a fact. Put away your book, Wally.

WALLY. Aw, Ma! By ten o'clock I got to know all about Canada.

MRS. WEBB. *(She sits and eats.)* You know the rules well as I do – no books at table. As for me, I'd rather have my children healthy than bright.

*(***WALLY** *puts book into bag, annoyed, then eats.)*

EMILY. I'm both, Mama: you know I am. I'm the brightest girl in school for my age. I have a wonderful memory.

MRS. WEBB. Eat your breakfast. *(rises and crosses for milk; returns to pour for both, replaces milk and sits)*

WALLY. I'm bright, too, when I'm looking at my stamp collection.

MRS. GIBBS. *(crosses to table and sets down butter)* I'll speak to your father about it when he's rested. Seems to me twenty-five cents a week's enough for a boy your age. *(crosses to stove to pour her own coffee)* I declare I don't know how you spend it all.

GEORGE. Aw, Ma – I gotta lotta things to buy.

MRS. GIBBS. Strawberry phosphates – that's what you spend it on. *(crosses between children with cup, sips)*

GEORGE. I don't see how Rebecca comes to have so much money. She has more'n a dollar.

REBECCA. *(spoon in mouth, dreamily)* I've been saving it up gradual.

MRS. GIBBS. Well, dear, I think it's a good thing to spend some every now and then.

REBECCA. Mama, do you know what I love most in the world – do you? – Money.

MRS. GIBBS. Eat your breakfast. *(crosses to set cup above the stove)*

(An old-fashioned schoolbell is heard in the distance.)

THE CHILDREN. Mama, there's first bell. – I gotta hurry. – I don't want any more. – I gotta hurry.

*(The **CHILDREN** rise, seize their books and dash out through the trellises. They meet, down center, and chattering, walk to Main Street, then turn left and exit.)*

*(The **STAGE MANAGER** goes off, unobtrusively, right.)*

MRS. WEBB. Walk fast, but you don't have to run. Wally, pull up your pants at the knee. Stand up straight, Emily. *(clears the table in two quick trips, putting dishes in the sink, then gets two bowls from under the sink)*

MRS. GIBBS. *(as the children start, following them a few steps out of the trellis)* Tell Miss Foster I send her my best congratulations – can you remember that?

REBECCA. Yes, Ma.

MRS. GIBBS. You look real nice, Rebecca. Pick up your feet.

ALL. Good-by.

*(**MRS. GIBBS** fills her apron with food for the chickens and comes down to the footlights.)*

(sounds of excited chickens)

MRS. GIBBS. *(feeding chickens)* Here, chick, chick, chick. No, go away, you. Go away. Here, chick, chick, chick. What's the matter with *you?* Fight, fight, fight, – that's all you do. Hm...*you* don't belong to me. Where'd you come from? *(flinging last of her feed, which causes loud clucks)*

(She shakes her apron.)

*(**MRS. WEBB**, laden with two large bowls, crosses through trellis, sits on bench and begins stringing beans.)*

MRS. GIBBS. Oh, don't be so scared. Nobody's going to hurt you. *(**MRS. GIBBS** turning to catch sight of **MRS. WEBB**)* Good morning, Myrtle. How's your cold?

MRS. WEBB. Well, I still get that tickling feeling in my throat. I told Charles I didn't know as I'd go to choir practice tonight. Wouldn't be any use.

MRS. GIBBS. Have you tried singing over your voice?

MRS. WEBB. Yes, but somehow I can't do that and stay on the key. While I'm resting myself I thought I'd string some of these beans.

MRS. GIBBS. *(rolling up her sleeves as she crosses the stage for a chat)* Let me help you. Beans have been good this year.

MRS. WEBB. I've decided to put up forty quarts if it kills me. The children say they hate 'em, but I notice they're able to get 'em down all winter.

(Pause. Brief sound of chickens cackling.)

MRS. GIBBS. Now, Myrtle. I've got to tell you something, because if I don't tell somebody I'll burst.

MRS. WEBB. Why, Julia Gibbs!

MRS. GIBBS. Here, give me some more of those beans. Myrtle, did one of those second-hand furniture men from Boston come to see you last Friday?

MRS. WEBB. No-o.

MRS. GIBBS. Well, he called on me. First I thought he was a patient wantin' to see Dr. Gibbs. 'N he wormed his way into my parlor, and, Myrtle Webb, *(both stop work)* he offered me three hundred and fifty dollars for Grandmother Wentworth's highboy, as I'm sitting here!

MRS. WEBB. Why, Julia Gibbs!

MRS. GIBBS. He did! That old thing! *(continues work)* Why, it was so big I didn't know where to put it and I almost give it to Cousin Hester Wilcox.

MRS. WEBB. Well, you're going to take it, aren't you?

MRS. GIBBS. I don't know.

MRS. WEBB. You don't know – three hundred and fifty dollars! What's come over you?

MRS. GIBBS. Well, if I could get the Doctor to take the money and go away someplace on a real trip, I'd sell it like that. *(stops work)* – Y'know, Myrtle, it's been the dream of my life to see Paris, France.

*(glances shyly at **MRS. WEBB**, who is shocked, then laughs, hand to face)*

– Oh, I don't know. It sounds crazy, I suppose, but for years I've been promising myself that if we ever had the chance –

MRS. WEBB. How does the Doctor feel about it?

MRS. GIBBS. *(continues to work through scene)* Well, I did beat about the bush a little and said that if I got a legacy – that's the way I put it – I'd make him take me somewhere.

MRS. WEBB. M-m-m…What did he say?

MRS. GIBBS. You know how he is. I haven't heard a serious word out of him since I've known him. No, he said, it might make him discontented with Grover's Corners to go traipsin' about Europe; better let well enough alone, he says. Every two years he makes a trip to the battlefields of the Civil War and that's enough treat for anybody, he says.

MRS. WEBB. Well, Mr. Webb just *admires* the way Dr. Gibbs knows everything about the Civil War. Mr. Webb's a good mind to give up Napoleon and move over to the Civil War, only Dr. Gibbs being one of the greatest experts in the country just makes him despair.

MRS. GIBBS. It's a fact! Dr. Gibbs is never so happy as when he's at Antietam or Gettysburg. The times I've walked over those hills, Myrtle, stopping at every bush and pacing it all out, like we were going to buy it.

MRS. WEBB. Well, if that second-hand man's really serious about buyin' it, Julia, you sell it. And then you'll get to see Paris, all right. Just keep droppin' hints from time to time – that's how I got to see the Atlantic Ocean, y'know.

MRS. GIBBS. Oh, I'm sorry I mentioned it. Only it seems to me that once in your life before you die you ought to see a country where they don't talk in English and don't even want to.

(The STAGE MANAGER *enters briskly from the right. He tips his hat to the ladies, who nod their heads.)*

STAGE MANAGER. Thank you, ladies. Thank you very much.

*(*MRS. GIBBS *and* MRS. WEBB *gather up their things, return into their homes and disappear.)*

Now we're going to skip a few hours. But first we want a little more information about the town, kind of a scientific account, you might say. So I've asked Professor Willard of our State University to sketch in a few details of our past history here. Is Professor Willard here?

(**PROFESSOR WILLARD**, *a rural savant, pince-nez on a wide satin ribbon, enters from the right with some notes in his hand.*)

May I introduce Professor Willard of our State University. A few brief notes, thank you, Professor, – unfortunately our time is limited.

PROFESSOR WILLARD. Grover's Corners...let me see... Grover's Corners lies on the old Pleistocene granite of the Appalachian range. I may say it's some of the oldest land in the world. We're very proud of that. A shelf of Devonian basalt crosses it with vestiges of Mesozoic shale, and some sandstone outcroppings; but that's all more recent: two hundred, three hundred million years old. Some highly interesting fossils have been found...I may say: unique fossils...two miles out of town, in Silas Peckham's cow pasture. They can be seen at the museum in our University at any time – that is, at any reasonable time. Shall I read some of Professor Gruber's notes on the meteorological situation – mean precipitation, et cetera?

STAGE MANAGER. Afraid we won't have time for that, Professor. We might have a few words on the history of man here.

PROFESSOR WILLARD. Yes...anthropological data: Early Amerindian stock. Cotahatchee tribes...no evidence before the tenth century of this era... hm...now entirely disappeared...possible traces in three families. Migration toward the end of the seventeenth century of English brachiocephalic blue-eyed stock...for the most part. Since then some Slav and Mediterranean –

STAGE MANAGER. And the population, Professor Willard?

PROFESSOR WILLARD. Within the town limits: 2,640.

STAGE MANAGER. Just a moment, Professor.

(He whispers into the **PROFESSOR***'s ear.)*

PROFESSOR WILLARD. Oh, yes, indeed? – The population, *at the moment,* is 2,642. The Postal District brings in 507 more, making a total of 3,149. – Mortality and birth rates: constant. – By MacPherson's gauge: 6.032.

STAGE MANAGER. Thank you very much, Professor. We're all very much obliged to you, I'm sure.

PROFESSOR WILLARD. Not at all, sir; not at all.

STAGE MANAGER. This way, Professor, and thank you again.

(Exit **PROFESSOR WILLARD***.)*

Now the political and social report: Editor Webb. – Oh, Mr. Webb?

(MRS. WEBB *appears at her back door.)*

MRS. WEBB. He'll be here in a minute…He just cut his hand while he was eatin' an apple.

STAGE MANAGER. Thank you, Mrs. Webb.

MRS. WEBB. Charles! Everybody's waitin'.

(Exit **MRS. WEBB***.)*

STAGE MANAGER. Mr. Webb is Publisher and Editor of the *Grover's Corners Sentinel.* That's our local paper, y'know.

(MR. WEBB *enters from his house, pulling on his coat. His finger is bound in a real handkerchief.)*

MR. WEBB. Well…I don't have to tell you that we're run here by a Board of Selectmen. – All males vote at the age of twenty-one. Women vote indirect. We're lower middle class: sprinkling of professional men…ten per cent illiterate laborers. Politically, we're eighty-six per cent Republicans; six per cent Democrats; four per cent Socialists; rest, indifferent. Religiously, we're eighty-five per cent Protestants; twelve per cent Catholics; rest, indifferent.

STAGE MANAGER. Have you any comments, Mr. Webb?

MR. WEBB. Very ordinary town, if you ask me. Little better behaved than most. Probably a lot duller. But our young people here seem to like it well enough. Ninety per cent of 'em graduating from high school settle down right here to live – even when they've been away to college.

STAGE MANAGER. Now, is there anyone in the audience who would like to ask Editor Webb anything about the town?

WOMAN IN THE BALCONY. Is there much drinking in Grover's Corners?

MR. WEBB. *(amused)* Well, ma'am, I wouldn't know what you'd call *much*. Satiddy nights the farmhands meet down in Ellery Greenough's stable and holler some. We've got one or two town drunks, but they're always having remorses every time an evangelist comes to town. No, ma'am, I'd say likker ain't a regular thing in the home here, except in the medicine chest. Right good for snake bite, y'know – always was.

BELLIGERENT MAN AT BACK OF AUDITORIUM. Is there no one in town aware of –

STAGE MANAGER. Come forward, will you, where we can all hear you – What were you saying?

BELLIGERENT MAN. Is there no one in town aware of social injustice and industrial inequality?

MR. WEBB. Oh, yes, everybody is – somethin' terrible. Seems like they spend most of their time talking about who's rich and who's poor.

BELLIGERENT MAN. Then why don't they do something about it?

(He withdraws without waiting for an answer.)

MR. WEBB. *(tolerantly)* Well, I dunno…I guess we're all hunting like everybody else for a way the diligent and sensible can rise to the top and the lazy and quarrelsome can sink to the bottom. But it ain't easy to find. Meanwhile, we do all we can to help those that can't help themselves and those that can we leave alone. – Are there any other questions?

LADY IN A BOX. Oh, Mr. Webb? Mr. Webb, is there any culture or love of beauty in Grover's Corners?

MR. WEBB. *(smiling)* Well, ma'am, there ain't much – not in the sense you mean. Come to think of it, there's some girls that play the piano at High School Commencement; but they ain't happy about it. No, ma'am, there isn't much culture; but maybe this is the place to tell you that we've got a lot of pleasures of a kind here: we like the sun comin' up over the mountain in the morning, and we all notice a good deal about the birds. We pay a lot of attention to them. And we watch the change of the seasons; yes, everybody knows about them. But those other things – you're right, ma'am, – there ain't much. – *Robinson Crusoe* and the Bible; and Handel's "Largo", we all know that; and Whistler's "Mother" – those are just about as far as we go.

LADY IN A BOX. So I thought. Thank you, Mr. Webb.

STAGE MANAGER. Thank you, Mr. Webb.

*(***MR. WEBB*** retires.)*

Now, we'll go back to the town. It's early afternoon. All 2,642 have had their dinners and all the dishes have been washed.

*(***MR. WEBB***, having removed his coat, returns and starts pushing a lawn mower to and fro beside his house.)*

There's an early-afternoon calm in our town: a buzzin' and a hummin' from the school buildings; only a few buggies on Main Street – the horses dozing at the hitching posts; you all remember what it's like. Doc Gibbs is in his office, tapping people and making them say "ah". Mr. Webb's cuttin' his lawn over there; one man in ten thinks it's a privilege to push his own lawn mower.

(Lights are now at high noon. Chicken sounds are again heard for a moment. Shrill girls' voices are heard, off left. **MR. WEBB** *kneels to pick grass from edge of walk.)*

No, sir. It's later than I thought. There are the children coming home from school already.

*(***EMILY*** *comes along Main Street, carrying some books. There are some signs that she is imagining herself to be a lady of startling elegance.)*

EMILY. I *can't*, Lois. I've got to go home and help my mother. I *promised*.

MR. WEBB. Emily, walk simply. Who do you think you are today?

EMILY. Papa, you're terrible. One minute you tell me to stand up straight and the next minute you call me names. I just don't listen to you.

(She gives him an abrupt kiss then strolls to the trellis.)

MR. WEBB. *(rising)* Golly, I never got a kiss from such a great lady before.

(He goes off pushing the lawn-mower. **EMILY** *leans over and picks some flowers by the gate of her house.)*

*(***GEORGE GIBBS*** *comes careening down Main Street. He is throwing a ball up to dizzying heights, and waiting to catch it again. This sometimes requires his taking six steps backward. He bumps into an* **OLD LADY** *invisible to us.)*

GEORGE. Excuse me, Mrs. Forrest.

STAGE MANAGER. *(as Mrs. Forrest)* Go out and play in the fields, young man. You got no business playing baseball on Main Street.

GEORGE. Awfully sorry, Mrs. Forrest.

(**STAGE MANAGER** *smiles at audience and drifts off downstage.* **GEORGE** *turns shyly, peering around the Webb house to see if* **EMILY** *is there.*)

– Hello, Emily.

EMILY. *(shyly turning from trellis)* H'lo.

GEORGE. *(edging down, socking mitt with baseball)* You made a fine speech in class.

EMILY. Well…I was really ready to make a speech about the Monroe Doctrine, but at the last minute Miss Corcoran made me talk about the Louisiana Purchase instead. I worked an awful long time on both of them.

GEORGE. *(puts ball back in pocket, looks at own house)* Gee, it's funny, Emily. From my window up there I can just see your head nights when you're doing your homework over in your room.

(**BOTH** *face mostly front, shy throughout.*)

EMILY. *(pleased at his admission)* Why, can you?

GEORGE. You certainly do stick to it, Emily. I don't see how you can sit still that long. I guess you like school.

EMILY. Well, I always feel it's something you have to go through.

GEORGE. Yeah.

EMILY. I don't mind it really. It passes the time.

GEORGE. Yeah. – Emily, what do you think? We might work out a kinda telegraph from your window to mine; and once in a while you could give me a kinda hint or two about one of those algebra problems.

(**EMILY** *looks at him, shocked.*)

I don't mean the answers, Emily, of course not… just some little hint…

EMILY. Oh, I think *hints* are allowed. – So – ah – if you get stuck, George, you whistle to me; and I'll give you some hints.

GEORGE. Emily, you're just naturally bright, I guess.

EMILY. I figure that it's just the way a person's born.

GEORGE. Yeah. But, you see, I want to be a farmer, and my Uncle Luke says whenever I'm ready I can come over and work on his farm and if I'm any good I can just gradually have it.

EMILY. You mean the house and everything?

*(Enter **MRS. WEBB** with a large bowl and sits on the bench by her trellis.)*

GEORGE. Yeah. *(Pause. Gets ball out; edges away.)* Well, thanks…I better be getting out to the baseball field. Thanks for the talk, Emily. – Good afternoon, Mrs. Webb.

*(**EMILY**, wrapt in thoughts of **GEORGE**, looks after him.)*

MRS. WEBB. Good afternoon, George.

GEORGE. So long, Emily.

(crosses off, socking ball into mitt)

EMILY. So long, George.

MRS. WEBB. Emily, come and help me string these beans for the winter.

*(**EMILY** sits and helps.)*

George Gibbs let himself have a real conversation, didn't he? Why, he's growing up. How old would George be?

EMILY. *(coming out of trance, protesting too much)* I don't know.

MRS. WEBB. Let's see. He must be almost sixteen.

EMILY. *(changing the subject)* Mama, I made a speech in class today and I was very good.

MRS. WEBB. You must recite it to your father at supper. What was it about?

EMILY. The Louisiana Purchase. It was like silk off a spool. I'm going to make speeches all my life. *(holding up a bean in both hands)* – Mama, are these big enough?

MRS. WEBB. Try and get them a little bigger if you can.

EMILY. Mama, will you answer me a question, serious?

MRS. WEBB. Seriously, dear – not serious.

EMILY. Seriously, – will you?

MRS. WEBB. Of course, I will.

EMILY. *(after a brief pause, expectantly)* Mama, am I good looking?

MRS. WEBB. *(steals a quick look at her)* Yes, of course you are. All my children have got good features; I'd be ashamed if they hadn't.

EMILY. Oh, Mama, that's not what I mean. What I mean is: am I *pretty?*

MRS. WEBB. I've already told you, yes. Now that's enough of that. You have a nice young pretty face. I never heard of such foolishness.

EMILY. Oh, Mama, you never tell us the truth about anything.

MRS. WEBB. I *am* telling you the truth.

EMILY. *(wheedling a bit)* Mama, were *you* pretty?

MRS. WEBB. Yes, I was, if I do say it. I was the prettiest girl in town next to Mamie Cartwright.

EMILY. But, Mama, you've got to say *some*thing about me. Am I pretty enough...to get anybody...to get people interested in me?

MRS. WEBB. *(turning on her, firmly)* Emily, you make me tired. Now stop it. You're pretty enough for all normal purposes. *(rises, taking bowl with her)* – Come along now and bring that bowl with you.

(She exits through trellis.)

EMILY. *(picking up bowl from floor and following)* Oh, Mama, you're no help at all.

(During preceding scene, the lights have gradually dimmed to late afternoon. Now they slowly change to night.)

STAGE MANAGER. *(appears with manuscript under his arm)* Thank you. Thank you! That'll do. We'll have to interrupt again here. Thank you, Mrs. Webb; thank you, Emily.

There are some more things we want to explore about this town.

(He comes to the center of the stage. During the following speech the lights gradually dim to darkness, leaving only a spot on him.)

I think this is a good time to tell you that the Cartwright interests have just begun building a new bank in Grover's Corners – had to go to Vermont for the marble, sorry to say. And they've asked a friend of mine what they should put in the cornerstone for people to dig up...a thousand years from now...Of course, they've put in a copy of *The New York Times* and a copy of Mr. Webb's *Sentinel*....We're kind of interested in this because some scientific fellas have found a way of painting all that reading matter with a glue – a silicate glue – that'll make it keep a thousand – two thousand years. We're putting in a Bible...and the Constitution of the United States – and a copy of William Shakespeare's plays. What do you say, folks? What do you think? Y'know – Babylon once had two million people in it, and all we know about 'em is the names of the kings and some copies of wheat contracts...and contracts for the sale of slaves. Yet every night all those families sat down to supper, and the father came home from his work, and the smoke went up the chimney, – same as here. And even in Greece and Rome, all we know about the *real* life of the people is what we can piece together out of the joking poems and the comedies they wrote for the theatre back then. So I'm going to have a copy of this play put in the cornerstone and the people a thousand years from now'll know a few simple facts about us – more than the Treaty of Versailles and the Lindbergh flight. See what I mean? So – people a thousand years from now – this is the way we were in the provinces north of New York at the beginning of the twentieth century. – This is the way we were: in our growing up and in our marrying and in our living and in our dying.

(A choir partially concealed in the orchestra pit has begun singing "Blessed Be the Tie That Binds".*)

(SIMON STIMSON *stands directing them.)*

(Two ladders have been pushed onto the stage; they serve as indication of the second story in the Gibbs and Webb houses. **GEORGE** *and* **EMILY** *mount them, and apply themselves to their schoolwork.)*

(DR. GIBBS *has entered and is seated in his kitchen reading.)*

STAGE MANAGER. *(cont.)* Well! – good deal of time's gone by. It's evening. You can hear choir practice going on in the Congregational Church. The children are at home doing their schoolwork. The day's running down like a tired clock.

(He listens a minute, then withdraws downstage.)

(At the end of the first line of the hymn, lights in the pit have come up showing the heads of the choir silhouetted as they face the stage, while **SIMON STIMSON** *conducts them, facing the audience, – now slightly drunk.)*

SIMON STIMSON. *(as verse ends)* Now look here, everybody. Music come into the world to give pleasure.

---

*This music appears on page 101 in the back of this Acting Edition.

(EMILY leans out the window and peers at GEORGE a moment, then works again.)

(Choir starts again, "Blessed Be the Tie That Binds" with increasing volume. At the end of the second phrase:)

(gently) Softer!

(They still increase in volume, and he suddenly becomes furious.)

Softer!

(Choir stops.)

Get it out of your heads that music's only good when it's loud. You leave loudness to the Methodists. You couldn't beat 'em, even if you wanted to. Now again. Tenors!

(Choir sings three verses of "Blessed Be the Tie That Binds".)

GEORGE. Hssst! Emily!

EMILY. Hello.

GEORGE. Hello!

EMILY. I can't work at all. The moonlight's so *terrible.*

GEORGE. Emily, did you get the third problem?

(DR. GIBBS comes downstairs and sits at the table, takes a book from it, reads.)

EMILY. Which?

GEORGE. The *third?*

EMILY. Why, yes, George – that's the easiest of them all.

GEORGE. I don't see it. Emily, can you give me a hint?

EMILY. I'll tell you one thing: the answer's in yards.

(First verse of hymn ends.)

GEORGE. *(!!!)* In yards? How do you mean?

EMILY. In *square* yards.

GEORGE. Oh…in square yards.

EMILY. Yes, George, don't you see?

GEORGE. Yeah. *(He does not see.)*

EMILY. In square yards of *wallpaper. (giving him more than a hint)*

GEORGE. Wallpaper *(a great light breaking)* – oh, I see.

(EMILY looks at him beaming agreement. He erases and rewrites.)

Thanks a lot, Emily.

EMILY. You're welcome. *(looks out)* My, isn't the moonlight *terrible?* And choir practice going on. *(listens hard a moment, awed)* – I think if you hold your breath you can hear the train all the way to Contoocook.

(GEORGE holds his breath, leaning out of the window.)

Hear it?

GEORGE. M-m-m – What do you know!

EMILY. Well, I guess I better go back and try to work.

GEORGE. Good night, Emily. And thanks.

EMILY. Good night, George.

(BOTH return unwillingly to work, but almost immediately give up and gaze at the moon, chins on hands.)

SIMON STIMSON. *(as the third verse ends)* Before I forget it: how many of you will be able to come in Tuesday afternoon and sing at Fred Hersey's wedding? – Show your hands.

(Choir raises hands. DR. GIBBS puts down book, ponders.)

That'll be fine; that'll be right nice. We'll do the same music we did for Jane Trowbridge's last month. – Now we'll do: "Art Thou Weary; Art Thou

Languid?" It's a question, ladies and gentlemen, make it talk. Ready.

(Choir sings two verses of "Art Thou Weary, Art Thou Languid?"*, the lights fading on them as they start.* **SIMON STIMSON** *disappears.)*

DR. GIBBS. *(calling offstage to upstairs)* Oh, George, can you come down a minute?

GEORGE. Yes, Pa.

(He descends the ladder.)

DR. GIBBS. Make yourself comfortable, George; I'll only keep you a minute.

*(***GEORGE*** sits.)*

George, how old are you?

GEORGE. I? I'm sixteen, almost seventeen.

DR. GIBBS. What do you want to do after school's over?

GEORGE. Why, you know, Pa. I want to be a farmer on Uncle Luke's farm.

DR. GIBBS. You'll be willing, will you, to get up early and milk and feed the stock...and you'll be able to hoe and hay all day?

GEORGE. Sure, I will. What are you...what do you mean, Pa?

DR. GIBBS. *(never harshly)* Well, George, while I was in my office today I heard a funny sound...and what do you think it was? It was your mother chopping wood.

*(***GEORGE*** turns slowly, ashamed.)*

DR. GIBBS. There you see your mother – getting up early; cooking meals all day long; washing and ironing; – and still she has to go out in the back yard and chop wood. I suppose she just got tired of asking you. She just gave up and decided it was

---

* This music appears on page 102 in the back of this Acting Edition.

easier to do it herself. And you eat her meals, and put on the clothes she keeps nice for you, and you run off and play baseball – like she's some hired girl we keep around the house but that we don't like very much.

(**GEORGE** *snivels.*)

Well, I knew all I had to do was call your attention to it. Here's a handkerchief, son.

(*Lays it on the table.* **GEORGE** *takes it, blows nose.*)

George, I've decided to raise your spending money twenty-five cents a week. Not, of course, for chopping wood for your mother, because that's a present you give her, but because you're getting older – and I imagine there are lots of things you must find to do with it.

GEORGE. Thanks, Pa.

DR. GIBBS. Let's see – tomorrow's your payday. You can count on it – Hmm. Probably Rebecca'll feel she ought to have some more too. Wonder what could have happened to your mother. Choir practice never was as late as this before.

GEORGE. (*still broken up*) It's only half past eight, Pa.

DR. GIBBS. I don't know why she's in that old choir. She hasn't any more voice than an old crow... Traipsin' around the streets at this hour of the night. (*finally, gently*) ...Just about time you retired, don't you think?

GEORGE. Yes, Pa. (*lays handkerchief by his father who pockets it*)

(**GEORGE** *mounts to his place on the ladder, gazes at the moon.* **DR. GIBBS** *soon resumes reading.*)

(*Laughter and good nights can be heard off stage left and presently* **MRS. GIBBS**, **MRS. SOAMES** *and* **MRS. WEBB** *come down Main Street. When they arrive at the corner of the stage they stop.*)

MRS. SOAMES. Good night, Martha. Good night, Mr. Foster.

(Women's voices respond.)

MRS. WEBB. *(calling off left)* I'll tell Mr. Webb; I *know* he'll want to put it in the paper.

MRS. GIBBS. My, it's late!

MRS. SOAMES. Good night, Irma.

(They stroll silently.)

MRS. GIBBS. Real nice choir practice, wa'n't it? Myrtle Webb! Look at that moon, will you! Tsk-tsk-tsk. Potato weather, for sure.

(They are silent a moment, gazing up at the moon.)

MRS. SOAMES. *(scandalized)* Naturally I didn't want to say a word about it in front of those others, *(looks offstage)* but now we're alone – really, it's the worst scandal that ever was in this town!

MRS. GIBBS. What?

MRS. SOAMES. Simon Stimson!

*(***MRS. WEBB*** *turns, annoyed.)*

MRS. GIBBS. Now, Louella!

MRS. SOAMES. But, Julia! To have the organist of a church *drink* and *drunk* year after year. You know he was drunk tonight.

MRS. GIBBS. Now, Louella! We all know about Mr. Stimson, and we all know about the troubles he's been through, and Dr. Ferguson knows too, and if Dr. Ferguson keeps him on there in his job the only thing the rest of us can do is just not to notice it.

MRS. SOAMES. *Not to notice it!* But it's getting worse.

MRS. WEBB. *(acidly)* No, it isn't, Louella. It's getting better. I've been in that choir twice as long as you have. It doesn't happen anywhere near so often...My, I hate to go to bed on a night like this. – I better hurry. Those children'll be sitting up till all hours. Good night, Louella.

(They all exchange good nights. She hurries downstage, enters her house and disappears.)

(EMILY, *as* **MRS. WEBB** *passes her, excitedly blows out – i.e., switches off – the light that shines on her face from the ladder-shelf, and again gazes at the moon.)*

MRS. GIBBS. Can you get home safe, Louella?

MRS. SOAMES. It's as bright as day. I can see Mr. Soames scowling at the window now. *(laughs at the thought)* You'd think we'd been to a dance the way the menfolk carry on.

(Both laugh and start on their ways.)

(More good nights. **MRS. GIBBS** *arrives at her home and passes through the trellis into the kitchen.)*

(GEORGE *snaps off the light on his ladder-shelf as his mother goes by.)*

MRS. GIBBS. Well, we had a real good time.

DR. GIBBS. *(looks at pocketwatch)* You're late enough.

MRS. GIBBS. Why, Frank, it ain't any later 'n usual.

DR. GIBBS. And you stopping at the corner to gossip with a lot of hens.

MRS. GIBBS. Now, Frank, don't be grouchy. Come out and smell the heliotrope in the moonlight.

(He puts book reluctantly on the table and rises. They stroll out arm in arm along the footlights.)

(A bobwhite calls three times. They speak quietly.)

Isn't that wonderful?

(They stop to survey the moonlit scene out front.)

What did you do all the time I was away?

DR. GIBBS. *(interested, though he tries to disapprove)* Oh, I read – as usual. What were the girls gossiping about tonight?

MRS. GIBBS. Well, believe me, Frank – there is something to gossip about.

DR. GIBBS. Hmm! Simon Stimson far gone, was he?

MRS. GIBBS. Worst I've ever seen him. How'll that end, Frank? Dr. Ferguson can't forgive him forever.

DR. GIBBS. I guess I know more about Simon Stimson's affairs than anybody in this town. Some people ain't made for small-town life. I don't know how that'll end; but there's nothing we can do but just leave it alone. *(pause)* Come, get in.

MRS. GIBBS. No, not yet...Frank, I'm worried about you.

DR. GIBBS. *(smiling)* What are you worried about?

MRS. GIBBS. I think it's my duty to make plans for you to get a real rest and change. And if I get that legacy, well, I'm going to insist on it.

DR. GIBBS. Now, Julia, there's no sense in going over that again.

MRS. GIBBS. Frank, you're just *unreasonable!*

DR. GIBBS. *(pats her back, pushes her, pouting, into the house)* Come on, Julia, it's getting late. First thing you know you'll catch cold. I gave George a piece of my mind tonight.

(Turns inside trelis to close door. **MRS. GIBBS** *picks up string from floor and, winding it up, goes to cupboard to leave it.)*

I reckon you'll have your wood chopped for a while anyway. No, no, start getting upstairs.

MRS. GIBBS. Oh, dear. There's always so many things to pick up, seems like. You know, Frank, Mrs. Fairchild always locks her front door every night.

*(***MRS. GIBBS** *starts upstairs and off.)*

All those people up that part of town do.

DR. GIBBS. *(blowing out the lamp)* They're all getting citified, that's the trouble with them. They haven't got nothing fit to burgle and everybody knows it.

(They disappear.)

(The sound of crickets. **REBECCA** *tiptoes to George's ladder and climbs up beside him.)*

GEORGE. Get out, Rebecca. There's only room for one at this window. You're always spoiling everything.

REBECCA. *(at the moon)* Well, let me look just a minute.

GEORGE. Use your own window.

REBECCA. I did, but there's no moon there…George, do you know what I think, do you? I think maybe the moon's getting nearer and nearer and there'll be a big 'splosion.

GEORGE. Rebecca, you don't know anything. If the moon were getting nearer, the guys that sit up all night with telescopes would see it first and they'd tell about it, and it'd be in all the newspapers. *(pause)*

REBECCA. George, is the moon shining on South America, Canada and half the whole world?

GEORGE. Well – prob'ly is.

(The **STAGE MANAGER** *strolls on.)*

*(***MR. WARREN***, an elderly policeman, comes along Main Street from the right, trying a door knob every few feet.* **MR. WEBB** *enters from the left.)*

(Pause. The sound of crickets is heard.)

STAGE MANAGER. Nine-thirty. Most of the lights are out. No, there's Constable Warren trying a few doors on Main Street. And here comes Editor Webb, after putting his newspaper to bed.

(Exits.)

MR. WEBB. Good evening, Bill.

CONSTABLE WARREN. Evenin', Mr. Webb.

MR. WEBB. Quite a moon!

CONSTABLE WARREN. *(looks at it, unmoved)* Yep.

(They stop to chat.)

MR. WEBB. All quiet tonight?

*(**SIMON STIMSON** comes down Main Street from the left, only a trace of unsteadiness in his walk.)*

CONSTABLE WARREN. Simon Stimson is rollin' around a little. Just saw his wife movin' out to hunt for him so I looked the other way – there he is now.

MR. WEBB. Good evening, Simon...Town seems to have settled down for the night pretty well....

*(**SIMON STIMSON** comes up to him and pauses a moment and stares at him, swaying slightly.)*

Good evening...Yes, most of the town's settled down for the night, Simon.... I guess we better do the same. Can I walk along a ways with you?

*(**SIMON STIMSON** continues on his way without a word and disappears at the right. Men turn to watch as he starts off.)*

Good night.

CONSTABLE WARREN. I don't know how that's goin' to end, Mr. Webb.

MR. WEBB. Well, he's seen a peck of trouble, one thing after another...Oh, Bill...if you see my boy smoking cigarettes, just give him a word, will you? He thinks a lot of you, Bill.

CONSTABLE WARREN. I don't think he smokes no cigarettes, Mr. Webb. Leastways, not more'n two or three a year.

MR. WEBB. Hm...I hope not. – Well, good night, Bill.

CONSTABLE WARREN. Good night, Mr. Webb.

(exits, trying doors)

MR. WEBB. *(stops right of ladder, sensing someone in window)* Who's that up there? Is that you, Myrtle?

EMILY. *(pooh-poohing him)* No, it's me, Papa.

MR. WEBB. Why aren't you in bed?

EMILY. I don't know. I just can't sleep yet, Papa. The moonlight's so *won*-derful. And the smell of Mrs. Gibbs' heliotrope. Can you smell it?

MR. WEBB. *(turns to smell, turns back)* Hm...Yes. Haven't any troubles on your mind, have you, Emily?

EMILY. *Troubles,* Papa? *No.*

MR. WEBB. Well, enjoy yourself, but don't let your mother catch you. Good night, Emily.

EMILY. Good night, Papa.

    *(***MR. WEBB*** crosses into the house, whistling "Blessed Be the Tie That Binds" and disappears.)*

REBECCA. *(when he is off, looking at the moon throughout)* I never told you about that letter Jane Crofut got from her minister when she was sick. He wrote Jane a letter and on the envelope the address was like this: It said: Jane Crofut; The Crofut Farm; Grover's Corners; Sutton County; New Hampshire; United States of America.

GEORGE. What's funny about that?

REBECCA. *(with increasing awe)* But listen, it's not finished: the United States of America; Continent of North America; Western Hemisphere; the Earth; the Solar System; the Universe; the Mind of God – that's what it said on the envelope.

GEORGE. What do you know!

REBECCA. And the postman brought it just the same.

GEORGE. What do you know!

    (Pause. Crickets.)

STAGE MANAGER. *(appearing down right)* That's the end of the First Act, friends. You can go and smoke now, those that smoke.

(The stage lights dim and **THE ACTORS** *walk off during the dim.)*

END OF ACT I

ACT II

(The tables and chairs of the two kitchens are still on the stage.)

(During intermission, the ladders and the small bench are withdrawn.)

(A minute before 'curtain time,' the stage lights fade gradually into an early morning blue.)

(The **STAGE MANAGER** *has been at his accustomed place watching the audience return to its seats.)*

(During the opening scene, morning light is gradually established.)

STAGE MANAGER. Three years have gone by. Yes, the sun's come up over a thousand times. Summers and winters have cracked the mountains a little bit more and the rains have brought down some of the dirt. Some babies that weren't even born before have begun talking regular sentences already; and a number of people who thought they were right young and spry have noticed that they can't bound up a flight of stairs like they used to, without their heart fluttering a little. All that can happen in a thousand days. Nature's been pushing and contriving in other ways, too: a number of young people fell in love and got married. Yes, the mountain got bit away a few fractions of an inch; millions of gallons of water went by the mill; and here and there a new home was set up under a roof. Almost everybody in the world gets married – you know what I mean? In our town there aren't hardly any exceptions. Most everybody in the world climbs into their graves married. The First Act was called the Daily Life. This act is called Love and Marriage. There's another act coming after this: I reckon you can guess what that's about. So: It's three years later. It's 1904. It's July 7th, just after High School Commencement. That's the time most of our young people jump up and get married. Soon as they've passed their last examinations in solid geometry and Cicero's Orations, looks like they suddenly feel themselves fit to be married. It's early morning.

(The sound of distant thunder.)

STAGE MANAGER. *(cont.)* Only this time it's been raining. It's been pouring and thundering. Mrs. Gibbs' garden, and Mrs. Webb's here: drenched. All those bean poles and pea vines: drenched. All yesterday over there on Main Street, the rain looked like curtains being blown along.

(More thunder. He looks up and out.)

Hm…it may begin again any minute.

(Distant train whistle. He looks at pocket watch.)

There! You can hear the 5:45 for Boston.

(MRS. GIBBS and MRS. WEBB enter their kitchens and start the day as in the First Act.)

(MRS. GIBBS again raises the shade and window and makes her wood fire. MRS. WEBB shakes the grate, adds coal to her stove, turns damper, fills coffee pot at sink.)

And there's Mrs. Gibbs and Mrs. Webb come down to make breakfast, just as though it were an ordinary day. I don't have to point out to the women in my audience that those ladies they see before them, both of those ladies cooked three meals a day – one of 'em for twenty years, the other for forty – and no summer vacation.

(MRS. WEBB crosses with pot to cupboard and grinds coffee.)

They brought up two children apiece, washed, cleaned the house – and *never a nervous breakdown.*

(**MRS. GIBBS** *grinds coffee into pot above stove.* **MRS. WEBB** *puts pot on stove and starts to make corn bread.*)

It's like what one of those Middle West poets said: You've got to love life to have life, and you've got to have life to love life…It's what they call a vicious circle.

HOWIE NEWSOME. (*offstage left*) Giddap, Bessie!

(*Sound of milk bottles in a rack starts off left and continues through scene as in Act I.* **MRS. GIBBS** *crosses to sink to pump water into a pot.*)

STAGE MANAGER. Here comes Howie Newsome delivering the milk.

(*Sound of newspapers slapping on verandahs off right.* **HOWIE** *starts down left, rack in hand.*)

And there's Si Crowell delivering the papers like his brother before him.

(**STAGE MANAGER** *watches a moment, then drifts off downstage.*)

(**MRS. GIBBS** *crosses to pump water into coffee pot.*)

(**SI CROWELL** *has entered hurling imaginary newspapers into doorways per Joe Crowell's routine in Act I;* **HOWIE NEWSOME** *has come along Main Street with Bessie.*)

SI CROWELL. Morning, Howie.

HOWIE NEWSOME. Morning, Si. – Anything in the papers I ought to know? (*Stops. Sets rack down.*)

(**MRS. GIBBS** *puts coffee on stove, crosses to cupboard and prepards two pieces of French toast. She holds back tears for a moment.* **MRS. WEBB** *crosses to cupboard to slice bacon and rearrange the shelves.*)

SI CROWELL. Nothing much, except we're losing about the best baseball pitcher Grover's Corners ever had – George Gibbs.

HOWIE NEWSOME. Reckon he is.

SI CROWELL. He could hit and run bases, too.

HOWIE NEWSOME. Yep. Mighty fine ball player.

(Horse whinny off left.)

(looking off left) – Whoa! Bessie! I guess I can stop and talk if I've a mind to!

SI CROWELL. I don't see how he could give up a thing like that just to get married. Would you, Howie?

HOWIE NEWSOME. Can't tell, Si. Never had no talent that way.

*(**CONSTABLE WARREN** enters. He walks with a cane, a little older than before. They exchange good mornings.)*

You're up early, Bill.

*(**MRS. GIBBS** puts French toast into skillet on stove, then gets cloth from cupboard, lays table, sets cup and plate for dog.)*

CONSTABLE WARREN. Seein' if there's anything I can do to prevent a flood. River's been risin' all night.

HOWIE NEWSOME. Si Crowell's all worked up here about George Gibbs' retiring from baseball.

CONSTABLE WARREN. Yes, sir; that's the way it goes. Back in '84 we had a player, Si – even George Gibbs couldn't touch him. Name of Hank Todd. Went down to Maine and become a parson. Wonderful ball player. – Howie, how does the weather look to you?

HOWIE NEWSOME. Oh, 'tain't bad. Think maybe it'll clear up for good.

*(**CONSTABLE WARREN** continues on his way.)*

*(**SI** starts off, throwing newspapers, exits.)*

*(**MRS. WEBB** puts bacon on stove, then washes and dries her hands at sink.)*

(HOWIE NEWSOME brings the milk first to MRS. GIBBS' house. She meets him by the trellis.)

MRS. GIBBS. Good morning, Howie. Do you think it's going to rain again?

HOWIE NEWSOME. *(sets down rack)* Morning, Mrs. Gibbs. It rained so heavy, I think maybe it'll clear up.

MRS. GIBBS. Certainly hope it will.

HOWIE NEWSOME. How much did you want today?

MRS. GIBBS. I'm going to have a houseful of relations, Howie. Looks to me like I'll need three-a-milk and two-a-cream.

HOWIE NEWSOME. *(handing her two bottles, putting three on the doorstep)* My wife says to tell you we both hope they'll be very happy, Mrs. Gibbs. Know they *will.*

(picks up rack, starts toward MRS. WEBB's house.)

MRS. GIBBS. *(calling after him)* Thanks a lot, Howie. Tell your wife I hope she gets there to the wedding.

(MRS. WEBB crosses down to trellis. MRS. GIBBS takes two bottles to cupboard, returns for other three, then crosses to turn French toast, winking back tears.)

HOWIE NEWSOME. Yes, she'll be there; she'll be there if she kin.

(HOWIE NEWSOME crosses to MRS. WEBB's house.)

Morning, Mrs. Webb. *(sets rack down)*

MRS. WEBB. Oh, good morning, Mr. Newsome. I told you four quarts of milk, but I hope you can spare me another.

HOWIE NEWSOME. *(kneeling, hands her two bottles, sets four on doorstep)* Yes'm…and the two of cream.

MRS. WEBB. *(looking up)* Will it start raining again, Mr. Newsome?

HOWIE NEWSOME. Well. Just sayin' to Mrs. Gibbs as how it may lighten up. *(rises, takes rack, starts up center)*

Mrs. Newsome told me to tell you as how we hope they'll both be very happy, Mrs. Webb. Know they *will*.

MRS. WEBB. *(calling after him)* Thank you, and thank Mrs. Newsome and we're counting on seeing you at the wedding.

HOWIE NEWSOME. Yes, Mrs. Webb. We hope to git there. Couldn't miss that. Come on, Bessie.

*(***HOWIE NEWSOME*** *exits.)*

*(***MRS. WEBB*** *takes two bottles to table above stove; returns for four more.* ***MRS. GIBBS*** *near stove stops to blow nose, on verge of tears.)*

*(***DR. GIBBS*** *descends in shirt sleeves, trying to be cheerful.)*

DR. GIBBS. Well, Ma, the day has come. You're losin' one of your chicks.

MRS. GIBBS. Frank Gibbs, don't you say another word. I feel like crying every minute. *(crosses to pour coffee at the table for him)* Sit down and drink your coffee.

*(***MRS. WEBB*** *peels and slices potatoes at table above stove.)*

DR. GIBBS. *(sits down at his breakfast table, tucks napkin into neck, puts sugar in coffee)* The groom's up shaving himself – only there ain't an awful lot to shave.

*(***MRS. GIBBS*** *sets pot on stove and crosses to cupboard for silver.)*

Whistling and singing, like he's glad to leave us. – Every now and then he says, "I do" to the mirror, but it don't sound convincing to me. *(blows coffee and drinks)*

MRS. GIBBS. *(crossing to table to set places for herself and Rebecca)* I declare, Frank, I don't know how he'll get along. I've arranged his clothes and seen to it he's put warm things on – Frank! They're too *young*. Emily won't think of such things. He'll catch his death of cold within a week.

DR. GIBBS. I was remembering my wedding morning, Julia.

MRS. GIBBS. *(crossing to stove to turn French toast)* Now don't start that, Frank Gibbs.

DR. GIBBS. *(smiling)* I was the scaredest young fella in the State of New Hampshire. I thought I'd make a mistake for sure.

*(**MRS. GIBBS** crosses to the cupboard to pour milk.)*

And when I saw you comin' down that aisle I thought you were the prettiest girl I'd ever seen, but the only trouble was that I'd never seen you before. There I was in the Congregational Church marryin' a total stranger.

*(**MRS. WEBB** sets table from cupboard in three trips.)*

MRS. GIBBS. *(crossing to table with milk for Rebecca)* And how do you think I felt! *(serves his toast)* – Frank, weddings are perfectly awful things. Farces, – that's what they are!

(She puts a plate before him.)

Here, I've made something for you.

DR. GIBBS. Why, Julia Hersey – French toast!

MRS. GIBBS. *(pleased)* 'Tain't hard to make and I had to do *something*. *(turns, suddenly serious, crosses to stove and serves self)*

*(Pause. **DR. GIBBS** pours on the syrup, round and round four times, then:)*

DR. GIBBS. How'd you sleep last night, Julia? *(eats)*

MRS. GIBBS. *(crossing to sit at table with own plate and coffee)* Well, I heard a lot of the hours struck off. *(takes sugar and cream)*

DR. GIBBS. *(thoughtfully)* Ye-e-s! I get a shock every time I think of George setting out to be a family man – that great gangling thing! – I tell you Julia, there's nothing so terrifying in the world as a *son*. The relation of father and son is the darndest, awkwardest –

MRS. GIBBS. *(stirs coffee)* Well, mother and daughter's no picnic, let me tell you. *(drinks)*

DR. GIBBS. They'll have a lot of troubles, I suppose, but that's none of our business. Everybody has a right to their own troubles.

(MRS. WEBB washes dishes.)

MRS. GIBBS. *(at the table, drinking her coffee, meditatively)* Yes…people are meant to go through life two by two. 'Tain't natural to be lonesome. *(cuts toast)*

(Pause. DR. GIBBS starts laughing.)

DR. GIBBS. Julia, do you know one of the things I was scared of when I married you?

MRS. GIBBS. Oh, go along with you! *(eats)*

DR. GIBBS. I was afraid we wouldn't have material for conversation more'n'd last us a few weeks.

(Both laugh.)

I was afraid we'd run out and eat our meals in silence, that's a fact. – Well, you and I been conversing for twenty years now without any noticeable barren spells. *(eats)*

(MRS. WEBB dries hands on towel.)

MRS. GIBBS. Well, – good weather, bad weather – 'tain't very choice, but I always find something to say. Did you hear Rebecca stirring around upstairs? *(Rises, taking both plates. Crosses to sink to scrape plates.)*

(MRS. WEBB crosses to sit at table, covers apron.)

DR. GIBBS. No. Only day of the year Rebecca hasn't been managing every-body's business up there.

She's hiding in her room. – I got the impression she's crying.

MRS. GIBBS. Lord's sakes! – This has got to stop. – Rebecca! Rebecca! Come and get your breakfast. (**DR. GIBBS** *wipes his mouth with napkin.*)

(**GEORGE** *comes rattling down the stairs, very brisk.*)

GEORGE. Good morning, everybody. Only five more hours to live. *(He makes the gesture of cutting his throat, and a loud "k-k-k", and starts through the trellis.)*

MRS. GIBBS. George Gibbs, where are you going?

GEORGE. *(stepping back into room)* Just stepping across the grass to see my girl.

MRS. GIBBS. Now, George! You put on your overshoes. It's raining torrents. You don't go out of this house without you're prepared for it.

(**DR. GIBBS** *rises, crosses to stairs, stops.*)

GEORGE. Aw, Ma. It's just a *step!*

MRS. GIBBS. George! You'll catch your death of cold and cough all through the service.

DR. GIBBS. George, do as your mother tells you!

(**DR. GIBBS** *goes upstairs.*)

(**GEORGE** *returns reluctantly to the kitchen and pantomimes putting on overshoes.*)

MRS. GIBBS. *(to cupboard for cup, sets it on table)* From tomorrow on you can kill yourself in all weathers, but while you're in my house you'll live wisely, thank you. *(crossing to stove for pot, starts to table with it)* – Maybe Mrs. Webb isn't used to callers at seven in the morning.

(**GEORGE** *rises, crosses into trellis.*)

MRS. GIBBS. *(cont.)* – Here, take a cup of coffee first.

GEORGE. Be back in a minute.

(He crosses the stage, leaping over the puddles.)

(MRS. GIBBS *shakes her head in annoyance, takes cup, pours coffee back in pot on stove, exits upstairs.)*

(crossing to her, cheerily) Good morning, Mother Webb.

MRS. WEBB. Goodness! You frightened me! *(rises, turns to him)* – Now, George, you can come in a minute out of the wet, but you know I can't ask you in.

GEORGE. Why not – ?

MRS. WEBB. George, you know 's well as I do: the groom can't see his bride on his wedding day, not until he sees her in church.

(enter **MR. WEBB***)*

GEORGE. Aw! – That's just a superstition. – Good morning, Mr. Webb.

MR. WEBB. Good morning, George. *(crosses to stove for coffee pot, takes it to table)*

GEORGE. *(laughing)* Mr. Webb, you don't believe in that superstition, do you?

MR. WEBB. There's a lot of common sense in some superstitions, George.

(He sits at the table.)

MRS. WEBB. *(pouring coffee for him)* Millions have folla'd it, George, and you don't want to be the first to fly in the face of custom. *(crosses to replace pot on stove)*

(MR. WEBB *takes four spoonfuls of sugar.)*

GEORGE. How is Emily?

MRS. WEBB. She hasn't waked up yet. I haven't heard a sound out of her. *(pouring coffee at stove)*

GEORGE. Emily's *asleep!!!*

MRS. WEBB. No wonder! We were up 'til all hours, sewing and packing. *(sets cup for* **GEORGE***)* Now I'll tell you what I'll do; you set down here a minute with Mr. Webb and drink this cup of coffee; *(crossing to stairs)* and I'll go upstairs and see she doesn't come down and surprise you. There's some bacon, too; but don't be long about it.

(Exit **MRS. WEBB.***)*

(Embarrassed silence. **GEORGE** *sits at table, uses sugar, stirs, steals look at* **MR. WEBB.***)*

*(***MR. WEBB** *dunks doughnuts in his coffee.)*

(more silence)

MR. WEBB. *(suddenly and loudly)* Well, George, how are you?

GEORGE. *(startled, choking over his coffee)* Oh, fine, I'm fine. *(Pause. Earnestly.)* Mr. Webb, what sense could there be in a superstition like that?

MR. WEBB. Well, you see – on her wedding morning a girl's head's apt to be full of...clothes and one thing and another. Don't you think that's probably it? *(dunks and eats)*

GEORGE. Ye-e-s. I never thought of that.

MR. WEBB. A girl's apt to be a mite nervous on her wedding day. *(pause)*

GEORGE. *(stirring coffee)* I wish a fellow could get married without all that marching up and down.

MR. WEBB. Every man that's ever lived has felt that way about it, George; but it hasn't been any use. It's the womenfolk who've built up weddings, my boy. For a while now the women have it all their own. A man looks pretty small at a wedding, George. All those good women standing shoulder to shoulder making sure that the knot's tied in a mighty public way. *(cuts food and eats)*

GEORGE. But...you *believe* in it, don't you, Mr. Webb?

MR. WEBB. *(With alacrity. Suddenly looking at* **GEORGE.***)* Oh, yes; *oh, yes.* Don't you misunderstand me, my boy. Marriage is a wonderful thing, – wonderful thing. And don't you forget that, George.

GEORGE. No, sir. *(pause)* Mr. Webb, how old were you when you got married?

MR. WEBB. Well, you see: I'd been to college and I'd taken a little time to get settled. But Mrs. Webb – she wasn't much older than what Emily is. *(stirring coffee)* Oh, age hasn't much to do with it, George – not compared with…uh…other things. *(drinks)*

GEORGE. What were you going to say, Mr. Webb?

MR. WEBB. Oh, I don't know. – Was I going to say something? *(pause)* George, I was thinking the other night of some advice my father gave me when I got married. Charles, he said, Charles, start out early showing who's boss, he said. Best thing to do is to give an order, even if it don't make sense; just so she'll learn to obey. And he said: if anything about your wife irritates you – her conversation, or anything – just get up and leave the house. That'll make it clear to her, he said. And, oh, yes! he said never, *never* let your wife know how much money you have, never.

GEORGE. Well, Mr. Webb…I don't think I could…

MR. WEBB. So I took the opposite of my father's advice and I've been happy ever since. And let that be a lesson to you, George, never to ask advice on personal matters. – George, are you going to raise chickens on your farm?

GEORGE. What?

MR. WEBB. Are you going to raise chickens on your farm?

GEORGE. *(hitches chair nearer, enthusiastic)* Uncle Luke's never been much interested, but I thought –

MR. WEBB. A book came into my office the other day, George, on the Philo System of raising chickens. I want you to read it. I'm thinking of beginning in a small way in the back yard, and I'm going to put an incubator in the cellar –

(**MRS. WEBB** *enters and crosses to* **MR. WEBB**.)

MRS. WEBB. Charles, are you talking about that old incubator again? I thought you two'd be talking about things worth while.

MR. WEBB. *(bitingly)* Well, Myrtle, if you want to give the boy some good advice, I'll go upstairs and leave you alone with him.

MRS. WEBB. *(pulling* **GEORGE** *up and forcing him through the trellis)* George, Emily's got to come downstairs and eat her breakfast. She sends you her love but she doesn't want to lay eyes on you. Good-by.

GEORGE. Good-by.

(**GEORGE** *crosses the stage to his own home, bewildered and crestfallen. He slowly dodges a puddle and disappears into his house.* **MRS. WEBB** *stands above the trellis, watching.*)

MR. WEBB. Myrtle, I guess you don't know about that older superstition.

MRS. WEBB. What do you mean, Charles?

MR. WEBB. *(wagging his finger)* Since the cave men: no bridegroom should see his father-in-law on the day of the wedding, or near it.

(exiting upstairs)

Now remember that.

(**MRS. WEBB**, *eyes following him in surprise, exits.*)

STAGE MANAGER. *(entering)* Thank you very much, Mr. and Mrs. Webb. – Now I have to interrupt again here. You see, we want to know how all this began – this wedding, this plan to spend a lifetime together. I'm awfully interested in how big things like that begin. You know how it is: you're twenty-one or twenty-two and you make some decisions; then whisssh! you're seventy: you've been a lawyer for fifty years, and that white-haired lady at your side has eaten over fifty thousand meals with you. How do such things begin? George and Emily are going to show you now the conversation they had when they first knew that...that...as the saying goes...they were meant for one another. But before they do it I want you to try and remember what it was like to have been very young. And particularly the days when you were first in love; when you were like a person sleepwalking, and you didn't quite see the street you were in, and didn't quite hear everything that was said to you. You're just a little bit crazy. Will you remember that, please? Now they'll be coming out of high school at three o'clock. George has just been elected President of the Junior Class, and as it's June, that means he'll be President of the Senior Class all next year. And Emily's just been elected Secretary and Treasurer.

(Young voices are heard off left.)

I don't have to tell you how important that is.

(Voices mount gaily as he places a board across the backs of two chairs, which he takes from those at the Gibbs family's table. He brings two high stools from the wings and places them behind the board. Persons sitting on the stools will be facing the audience. This is the counter of Mr. Morgan's drugstore. **STAGE MANAGER** *exits.)*

Yep – there they are coming down Main Street now.

*(***EMILY***, carrying an armful of – imaginary – schoolbooks, comes along Main Street from the left, speaking off left as voices die out.)*

EMILY. I can't, Louise. I've got to go home. Good-by. Oh, Ernestine! Ernestine! Can you come over tonight and do Latin? Isn't that Cicero the worst thing – ! Tell your mother you *have* to. G'by. G'by, Helen. G'by, Fred.

(**GEORGE,** *also carrying books, catches up with her.*)

GEORGE. Can I carry your books home for you, Emily?

EMILY. *(coolly)* Why…uh…Thank you. It isn't far.

(She gives them to him. **GEORGE** *takes her books under his arm, turns to speak offstage.* **EMILY** *is shy and embarrassed.)*

GEORGE. Excuse me a minute, Emily. *(hurriedly)* Say, Bob, if I'm a little late, start practice anyway. And give Herb some long high ones.

EMILY. *(suddenly alert)* Good-by, Lizzy.

GEORGE. *(also to "Lizzy", not enthusiastic)* Good-by, Lizzy.
– I'm awfully glad you were elected, too, Emily.

EMILY. *(coolly)* Thank you.

(They have been standing on Main Street, almost against the back wall. They take the first steps toward the audience when **GEORGE** *stops and says:)*

GEORGE. *(hurt)* Emily, why are you mad at me?

EMILY. *(defensive)* I'm not mad at you.

GEORGE. You've been treating me so funny lately.

EMILY. *(dreading to face the issue)* Well, since you ask me, I might as well say it right out, George, –

(She catches sight of a teacher passing.)

Good-by, Miss Corcoran.

GEORGE. Good-by, Miss Corcoran. – Wha – what is it?

EMILY. *(not scoldingly; finding it difficult to say)* I don't like the whole change that's come over you in the last year.

*(**GEORGE** turns away, a bit hurt. She glances at him.)*

I'm sorry if that hurts your feelings, but I've got to – tell the truth and shame the devil.

GEORGE. A *change?* – Wha – what do you mean?

EMILY. Well, up to a year ago I used to like you a lot. And I used to watch you as you did everything... because we'd been friends so long...and then you began spending all your time at *baseball* ...and you never stopped to speak to anybody any more. Not even to your own family you didn't...and, George, it's a fact, you've got awful conceited and stuck-up, and all the girls say so. They may not say so to your face, but that's what they say about you behind your back, and it hurts me to hear them say it, but I've got to agree with them a little. I'm sorry if it hurts your feelings...but I can't be sorry I said it.

GEORGE. *(helpless and hurt)* I...I'm glad you said it, Emily. I never thought that such a thing was happening to me. I guess it's hard for a fella not to have faults creep into his character.

(They take a step or two in silence, then stand still in misery.)

EMILY. I always expect a man to be perfect and I think he should be.

GEORGE. Oh...I don't think it's possible to be perfect, Emily.

EMILY. *(all innocence, yet firm)* Well, my *father* is, and as far as I can see *your* father is. There's no reason on earth why you shouldn't be, too.

GEORGE. Well, I feel it's the other way round. That men aren't naturally good; but girls are.

EMILY. Well, you might as well know right now that I'm not perfect. It's not as easy for a girl to be perfect as a man, because we girls are more – more – nervous. – Now I'm sorry I said all that about you. I don't know what made me say it. *(cries)*

GEORGE. *(choked voice)* Emily, –

EMILY. Now I can see it's not the truth at all. And I suddenly feel that it isn't important, anyway.

GEORGE. Emily...would you like an ice-cream soda, or something, before you go home?

EMILY. *(controlling herself)* Well, thank you...I would.

*(**GEORGE** starts to take her arm, but is too shy. They advance toward the audience and make an abrupt right turn, opening the door of Morgan's drugstore. Under strong emotion, **EMILY** keeps her face down. **GEORGE** speaks to some passers-by.)*

GEORGE. Hello, Stew, – how are you? – Good afternoon, Mrs. Slocum.

*(**GEORGE** starts into store, then steps back to let **EMILY** go first. They cross to stools and **GEORGE** puts books down on board.)*

*(The **STAGE MANAGER**, wearing spectacles and assuming the role of Mr. Morgan, enters abruptly from the right and stands between the audience and the counter of his soda fountain.)*

STAGE MANAGER. Hello, George. Hello, Emily. – What'll you have? – Why, Emily Webb, – what you been crying about?

GEORGE. *(He gropes for an explanation.)* She...she just got an awful scare, Mr. Morgan. She almost got run over by that hardware-store wagon. Everybody says that Tom Huckins drives like a crazy man.

STAGE MANAGER. *(drawing a drink of water)* Well, now! You take a drink of water, Emily.

*(**EMILY** and **GEORGE** sit on stools.)*

You look all shook up. I tell you, you've got to look both ways before you cross Main Street these days.

(Sets glass before her. She sips.)

Gets worse every year. – What'll you have?

EMILY. I'll have a strawberry phosphate, thank you, Mr. Morgan.

GEORGE. No, no, Emily. Have an ice-cream soda with me. Two strawberry ice-cream sodas, Mr. Morgan.

STAGE MANAGER. *(working the faucets)* Two strawberry ice-cream sodas, yes sir. Yes, sir. There are a hundred and twenty-five horses in Grover's Corners this minute I'm talking to you.

State Inspector was in here yesterday. And now they're bringing in these auto-mo-biles, the best thing to do is to just stay home. Why, I can remember when a dog could go to sleep all day in the middle of Main Street and nothing come along to disturb him.

(He sets the imaginary glasses before them.)

There they are. Enjoy 'em.

(He sees a customer, right.)

Yes, Mrs. Ellis. What can I do for you?

(He goes out right.)

EMILY. They're so expensive. *(sips through straw)*

GEORGE. No, no, – don't you think of that. We're celebrating our election. And then do you know what else I'm celebrating?

EMILY. N-no.

GEORGE. I'm celebrating because I've got a friend who tells me all the things that ought to be told me.

EMILY. George, *please* don't think of that. I don't know why I said it. It's not true. You're –

GEORGE. *(with a brief look at her)* No, Emily, you stick to it. I'm glad you spoke to me like you did. But you'll *see:* I'm going to change so quick – you bet I'm going to change. And, Emily, I want to ask you a favor.

EMILY. What?

GEORGE. Emily, if I go away to State Agriculture College next year...will you write me a letter once in a while?

EMILY. I certainly will. I certainly will, George...

(Pause. They start sipping the sodas through the straws.)

It certainly seems like being away three years you'd get out of touch with things. Maybe letters from Grover's Corners wouldn't be so interesting after a while. Grover's Corners isn't a very important place when you think of all – New Hampshire; but I think it's a very nice town.

GEORGE. The day wouldn't come when I wouldn't want to know everything that's happening here. I know *that's* true, Emily.

EMILY. Well, I'll try to make my letters interesting. *(pause)*

GEORGE. Y'know. Emily, whenever I meet a farmer I ask him if he thinks it's important to go to Agriculture School to be a good farmer.

EMILY. *(looks at him, happy that he might not leave town)* Why, George –

GEORGE. *(eagerly)* Yeah, and some of them say that it's even a waste of time. You can get all those things, anyway, out of the pamphlets the government sends out. And Uncle Luke's getting old, – he's about ready for me to start in taking over his farm tomorrow, if I could.

EMILY. *(glowing)* My!

GEORGE. And, like you say, being gone all that time... in other places and meeting other people...Gosh, if anything like that can happen I don't want to go away. I guess new people aren't any better than old ones. I'll bet they almost never are. Emily...I feel that you're as good a friend as I've got. I don't need to go and meet the people in other towns.

EMILY. *(to him, arguing nobly against her inclinations)* But, George, maybe it's very important for you to go and learn all that about – cattle judging and soils and those things...Of course, I don't know.

GEORGE. *(after a pause, very seriously)* Emily, I'm going to make up my mind right now. I won't go. I'll tell Pa about it tonight.

EMILY. Why, George, I don't see why you have to decide right now. It's a whole year away.

GEORGE. Emily, I'm glad you spoke to me about that... that fault in my character. What you said was right; but there was *one* thing wrong in it, and that was when you said that for a year I wasn't noticing people, and...you, for instance. Why, you say you were watching me when I did everything...I was doing the same about you all the time.

(She looks at him wide-eyed, he at her.)

Why, sure, – I always thought about you as one of the chief people I thought about. I always made sure where you were sitting on the bleachers, and who you were with, and for three days now I've been trying to walk home with you; but something's always got in the way. Yesterday I was standing over against the wall waiting for you, and you walked home with *Miss Corcoran.*

EMILY. George!...Life's awful funny! How could I have known that? Why, I thought –

GEORGE. Listen, Emily, I'm going to tell you why I'm not going to Agriculture School. I think that once you've found a person that you're very fond of...I mean a person who's fond of you, too, and likes you enough to be interested in your character... Well, I think that's just as important as college is, and even more so. That's what I think.

EMILY. *(quietly)* I think it's awfully important, too. *(pause)*

GEORGE. Emily.

EMILY. Y-yes, George.

GEORGE. Emily, if I *do* improve and make a big change...would you be...I mean: *could* you be...

EMILY. I...I am now; I always have been.

GEORGE. *(pause)* So I guess this is an important talk we've been having.

EMILY. Yes…yes.

GEORGE. *(takes a deep breath and straightens his back)* Wait just a minute and I'll walk you home.

(Both rise.)

(With mounting alarm, he digs into his pockets for the money.)

(The **STAGE MANAGER** *enters, right.)*

(GEORGE, *deeply embarrassed, but direct, says to him:)*

Mr. Morgan, I'll have to go home and get the money to pay you for this. It'll only take me a minute.

STAGE MANAGER. *(pretending to be affronted)* What's that? George Gibbs, do you mean to tell me – !

GEORGE. Yes, but I had reasons, Mr. Morgan. – Look, here's my gold watch to keep until I come back with the money.

STAGE MANAGER. That's all right. Keep your watch. I'll trust you.

GEORGE. I'll be back in five minutes.

STAGE MANAGER. I'll trust you ten years, George, – not a day over.

(GEORGE *slowly gets the point – laughs, returns watch.)*

– Got all over your shock, Emily?

EMILY. Yes, thank you, Mr. Morgan. It was nothing.

GEORGE. *(taking up the books from the counter)* I'm ready.

(They walk in grave silence across the stage and pass through the trellis at the Webbs' back door and disappear.)

(The **STAGE MANAGER** *watches them go out, then turns to the audience, removing his spectacles.)*

STAGE MANAGER. Well, – *(He claps his hands as a signal.)* Now we're ready to get on with the wedding.

(Immediately the lights, except a pinspot which covers him, fade out.)

(He stands waiting while the set is prepared for the next scene.)

(STAGEHANDS remove the chairs, tables and trellises from the Gibbs and Webb houses.)

(They arrange more chairs, facing up, on either side of the aisle, in close formation to suggest the pews of a church. The congregation will sit facing the back wall. The aisle of the church starts at the center of the back wall and comes toward the audience.)

(A small platform is placed against the back wall on which the STAGE MANAGER will stand later, playing the minister.)

(The image of a stained-glass window is cast upon the back wall.)

(When all is ready the STAGE MANAGER strolls to the center of the stage, down front, and, musingly, addresses the audience.)

STAGE MANAGER. There are a lot of things to be said about a wedding; there are a lot of thoughts that go on during a wedding. We can't get them all into one wedding, naturally, and especially not into a wedding at Grover's Corners, where they're awfully plain and short. In this wedding I play the minister. That gives me the right to say a few more things about it. For a while now, the play gets pretty serious. Y'see, some churches say that marriage is a sacrament. I don't quite know what that means, but I can guess. Like Mrs. Gibbs said a few minutes ago: People were made to live two-by-two. This is a good wedding, but people are so put together that even at a good wedding there's a lot of confusion way down deep in people's minds and we thought that that ought to be in our play, too. The real hero of this scene isn't on the stage at all, and you know who that is. It's like what one of those European fellas said: every child born into the world is nature's attempt to make a perfect human being. Well, we've seen nature pushing and contriving for some time now. We all know that nature's interested in quantity; but I think she's interested in quality, too, – that's why I'm in the ministry. And don't forget all the other witnesses at this wedding, – the ancestors. Millions of them. Most of them set out to live two-by-two, also. Millions of them. Well, that's all my sermon. 'Twan't very long, anyway. *(Turning upstage, he walks up the church aisle.)*

(The organ starts playing Handel's "Largo".)

(The congregation streams into the church and sits in silence.)

(Church bells are heard.)

*(***MRS. GIBBS*** *sits in the front row, the first seat on the aisle, the right section; next to her are* **REBECCA** *and* **DR. GIBBS**.*)

(Across the aisle **MRS. WEBB**, **WALLY** *and* **MR. WEBB**. *A small choir takes its place, facing the audience under the stained-glass window.)*

*(***MRS. WEBB**, *on the way to her place, turns back and speaks to the audience.)*

MRS. WEBB. I don't know why on earth I should be crying. I suppose there's nothing to cry about. It came over me at breakfast this morning; there was Emily eating her breakfast as she's done for seventeen years and now she's going off to eat it in someone else's house. I suppose that's it. And

Emily! She suddenly said: I can't eat another mouthful, and she put her head down on the table and *she* cried. *(She starts toward her seat in the church, but turns back and adds:)* Oh, I've got to say it: you know, there's something downright cruel about sending our girls out into marriage this way. I hope some of her girl friends have told her a thing or two. It's cruel, I know, but I couldn't bring myself to say anything. I went into it blind as a bat myself. *(in half-amused exasperation)* The whole world's wrong, that's what's the matter. There they come.

(She hurries to her place in the pew, sees **GEORGE** *start to come down the right aisle of the theatre, through the audience.)*

(Suddenly **THREE MEMBERS** *of his baseball team appear downstage right and start whistling and catcalling to him. They are dressed for the ball field.)*

THE BASEBALL PLAYERS. Eh, George, George! Hast – yaow! Look at him, fellas – he looks scared to death. Yaow! George, don't look so innocent, you old geezer. We know what you're thinking. Don't disgrace the team, big boy. Whoo-oo-oo.

STAGE MANAGER. All right! All right! That'll do. That's enough of that.

(Smiling, he pushes them off the stage. They lean back to shout a few more catcalls.)

There used to be an awful lot of that kind of thing at weddings in the old days, – Rome, and later. We're more civilized now, – so they say.

(The choir starts singing "Love Divine, All Loves Excelling". * **GEORGE** *has reached the stage having come down the stage right aisle. He stares at*

---

* This music appears on page 102 in the back of this Acting Edition.

the congregation a moment, then takes a few steps of withdrawal, toward the right proscenium pillar. His mother, from the front row, seems to have felt his confusion. She leaves her seat and comes down the aisle quickly to him.)

MRS. GIBBS. George! George! What's the matter?

GEORGE. Ma, I don't want to grow old. Why's everybody pushing me so?

MRS. GIBBS. Why, George…you wanted it.

GEORGE. No, Ma, listen to me –

MRS. GIBBS. No, no, George, – you're a man now.

GEORGE. Listen, Ma, – for the last time I ask you…All I want to do is to be a fella –

MRS. GIBBS. George! If anyone should hear you! Now stop. Why, I'm ashamed of you!

*(**GEORGE** comes to himself and looks over the scene.)*

GEORGE. What? Where's Emily?

MRS. GIBBS. *(relieved)* George! You gave me such a turn.

GEORGE. Cheer up, Ma. I'm getting married.

MRS. GIBBS. Let me catch my breath a minute.

GEORGE. *(comforting her)* Now, Ma, you save Thursday nights. Emily and I are coming over to dinner every Thursday night…you'll see. Ma, what are you crying for? Come on; we've got to get ready for this.

*(**MRS. GIBBS**, mastering her emotion, fixes his tie and whispers to him.)*

*(In the meantime, **EMILY**, in white and wearing her wedding veil, has come through the audience and mounted onto the stage. She too draws back, frightened, when she sees the congregation in the church. As **EMILY** appears, the choir begins: "Blessed Be the Tie That Binds".)*

EMILY. I never felt so alone in my whole life.

(**MR. WEBB**, *hearing her, leaves his seat in the pews and comes toward her anxiously.*)

And George over there, looking so…! I *hate* him. I wish I were dead. Papa! Papa! *(flings herself into his arms)*

MR. WEBB. Emily! Emily! Now don't get upset….

EMILY. But, Papa, – I don't want to get married….

MR. WEBB. Sh – sh – Emily. Everything's all right.

EMILY. *(pleading)* Why can't I stay for a while just as I am? Let's go away, –

MR. WEBB. No, no, Emily. Now stop and think a minute.

EMILY. Don't you remember that you used to say, – all the time you used to say – all the time: that I was *your* girl! There must be lots of places we can go to. I'll work for you. I could keep house.

MR. WEBB. Sh…You mustn't think of such things. You're just nervous, Emily. *(He turns and calls:)* George! George! Will you come here a minute?

(*He leads her toward* **GEORGE**. **GEORGE** *crosses to meet them.*)

Why you're marrying the best young fellow in the world. George is a fine fellow.

EMILY. But Papa, –

(**MRS. GIBBS**, *returns unobtrusively to her seat.*)

(**MR. WEBB** *has one arm around his daughter. He places his hand on* **GEORGE**'s *shoulder.*)

MR. WEBB. I'm giving away my daughter, George. Do you think you can take care of her?

GEORGE. *(trembling)* Mr. Webb, I want to…I want to try.

(**MR. WEBB** *turns to face up, blows his nose.* **EMILY** *and* **GEORGE** *face each other, helpless, breathless.*)

Emily, I'm going to do my best. I love you, Emily. I need you.

EMILY. Well, if you love me, help me. All I want is someone to love me.

GEORGE. I will, Emily. Emily, I'll try.

EMILY. And I mean for *ever.* Do you hear? Forever and ever.

(They fall into each other's arms.)

("The March" from Lohengrin is heard.)

(The **STAGE MANAGER,** *as* **CLERGYMAN,** *stands on the box, up center.)*

MR. WEBB. Come, they're waiting for us. Now you know it'll be all right. Come, quick.

*(***GEORGE** *slips away and takes his place beside the* **STAGE MANAGER-CLERGYMAN.** *)*

*(***EMILY** *proceeds up the aisle on her father's arm.)*

*(***MR. WEBB** *arrives at the pulpit with* **EMILY,** *leaves her facing* **GEORGE** *and goes to his seat. The crowd has bustled with interest during* "The March" *and is now all attention.)*

STAGE MANAGER. Do you, George, take this woman, Emily, to be your wedded wife, to have...

(His voice sinks to an unintelligible mumble over which rises the voice of **MRS. SOAMES.** *)*

*(***MRS. SOAMES** *has been sitting in the last row of the congregation.)*

(She now turns to her neighbors and speaks in a shrill voice. Her chatter drowns out the rest of the clergyman's words.)

MRS. SOAMES. Perfectly lovely wedding! Loveliest wedding I ever saw. Oh, I do love a good wedding, don't you? Doesn't she make a lovely bride?

GEORGE. I do.

STAGE MANAGER. Do you, Emily, take this man, George, to be your wedded husband, –

(Again his further words are covered by those of **MRS. SOAMES**.*)*

MRS. SOAMES. Don't know *when* I've seen such a lovely wedding. But I always cry. Don't know why it is, but I always cry. I just like to see young people happy, don't you? Oh, I think it's lovely.

(The **STAGE MANAGER** *mutters, "The Ring."* **GEORGE** *takes it from his pocket, slips it on* **EMILY**'s *finger, then steps to embrace and kiss her.)*

(The stage is suddenly arrested into silent tableau.)

(The **STAGE MANAGER**, *his eyes on the distance, as though to himself:)*

STAGE MANAGER. I've married over two hundred couples in my day. Do I believe in it? I don't know. M…marries N… millions of them. The cottage, the go-cart, the Sunday-afternoon drives in the Ford, the first rheumatism, the grandchildren, the second rheumatism, the deathbed, the reading of the will, –

(He now looks at the audience for the first time, with a warm smile that removes any sense of cynicism from the next line.)

Once in a thousand times it's interesting. – Well, let's have Mendelssohn's "Wedding March"!

(The organ picks up the March. Church bells sound.)

(The **BRIDE** *and* **GROOM** *come down the aisle, radiant, but trying to be very dignified.)*

(The **TOWNSPEOPLE** *have gradually risen and turned to watch as they pass by, chattering.)*

MRS. SOAMES. *(as "Wedding March" starts)* Aren't they a lovely couple? Oh, I've never been to such a nice wedding. I'm sure they'll be happy. I always say:

happiness, that's the great thing! The important thing is to be happy.

(The **BRIDE** *and* **GROOM** *reach the steps leading into the audience. A bright light is thrown upon them. They descend into the auditorium and run up the aisle joyously.)*

STAGE MANAGER. That's all the Second Act, folks. Ten minutes' intermission.

(Lights fade. **STAGE MANAGER** *in momentary darkness walks off. The crowd exits.)*

ACT III

(During the intermission the audience has seen the stagehands arranging the stage. On the right-hand side, a little right of the center, ten or twelve ordinary chairs have been placed in three openly spaced rows facing the audience.)

(These are graves in the cemetery.)

*(Toward the end of the intermission the **ACTORS** enter and take their places. The front row contains: toward the center of the stage, an empty chair; then **MRS. GIBBS;** **SIMON STIMSON**.)*

*(The second row contains, among others, **MRS. SOAMES**.)*

*(The third row has **WALLY WEBB**.)*

(The dead do not turn their heads or their eyes to right or left, but they sit in a quiet without stiffness. When they speak their tone is matter-of-fact, without sentimentality and, above all, without lugubriousness.)

*(The **STAGE MANAGER** takes his accustomed place and waits for the house lights to go down.)*

STAGE MANAGER. This time nine years have gone by, friends – summer, 1913. Gradual changes in Grover's Corners. Horses are getting rarer. Farmers coming into town in Fords. Everybody locks their house doors now at night. Ain't been any burglars in town yet, but everybody's heard about 'em. You'd be surprised, though – on the whole, things don't change much around here. This is certainly an important part of Grover's Corners.

It's on a hilltop – a windy hilltop – lots of sky, lots of clouds, – often lots of sun and moon and stars. You come up here, on a fine afternoon and you can see range on range of hills – awful blue they are – up there by Lake Sunapee and Lake Winnipesaukee… and way up, if you've got a glass, you can see the White Mountains and Mt. Washington – where North Conway and Conway is. And, of course, our favorite mountain, Mt. Monadnock's right here – and all these towns that lie around it: Jaffrey, 'n East Jaffrey, 'n Peterborough, 'n Dublin; and *(then pointing down in the audience)* there, quite a ways down, is Grover's Corners. Yes, beautiful spot up here. Mountain laurel and li-lacks. I often wonder why people like to be buried in Woodlawn and Brooklyn when they might pass the same time up here in New Hampshire. Over there – *(pointing to stage left)* are the old stones, – 1670, 1680. Strong-minded people that come a long way to be independent. Summer people walk around there laughing at the funny words on the tombstones… it don't do any harm. And genealogists come up from Boston – get paid by city people for looking up their ancestors. They want to make sure they're Daughters of the American Revolution and of the *Mayflower*…Well, I guess that don't do any harm, either. Wherever you come near the human race, there's layers and layers of nonsense… Over there are some Civil War veterans. Iron flags on their graves…New Hampshire boys…had a notion that the Union ought to be kept together, though they'd never seen more than fifty miles of it themselves. All they knew was the name, friends – the United States of America. The United States of America. And they went and died about it. This here is the new part of the cemetery. Here's your friend Mrs. Gibbs. 'N let me see – Here's Mr. Stimson, organist at the Congregational Church.

And Mrs. Soames who enjoyed the wedding so
– you remember? Oh, and a lot of others. And
Editor Webb's boy, Wallace, whose appendix burst
while he was on a Boy Scout trip to Crawford
Notch. Yes, an awful lot of sorrow has sort of
quieted down up here. People just wild with grief
have brought their relatives up to this hill. We all
know how it is...and then time...and sunny days...
and rainy days...'n snow...We're all glad they're
in a beautiful place and we're coming up here
ourselves when our fit's over. Now there are some
things we all know, but we don't take'm out and
look at'm very often. We all know that *something*
is eternal. And it ain't houses and it ain't names,
and it ain't earth, and it ain't even the stars...
everybody knows in their bones that *something* is
eternal, and that something has to do with human
beings. All the greatest people ever lived have
been telling us that for five thousand years and yet
you'd be surprised how people are always losing
hold of it. There's something way down deep
that's eternal about every human being. *(pause)*
You know as well as I do that the dead don't
stay interested in us living people for very long.
Gradually, gradually, they lose hold of the earth...
and the ambitions they had...and the pleasures
they had...and the things they suffered...and the
people they loved. They get weaned away from
earth – that's the way I put it, – weaned away. And
they stay here while the earth part of 'em burns
away, burns out; and all that time they slowly get
indifferent to what's goin' on in Grover's Corners.
They're waitin'. They're waitin' for something
that they feel is comin'. Something important,
and great. Aren't they waitin' for the eternal part
in them to come out clear? Some of the things
they're going to say maybe'll hurt your feelings
– but that's the way it is: mother 'n daughter...

husband 'n wife…enemy 'n enemy…money 'n miser…all those terribly important things kind of grow pale around here. And what's left when memory's gone, and your identity, Mrs. Smith?

(He looks at the audience a minute, then turns to the stage.)

(JOE STODDARD, *60-odd, enters, crossing to glance at a grave a moment, then turns downstage a bit and stands watching for mourners off left. He carries his hat. At the same time,* **SAM CRAIG**, *30, enters, wiping his forehead from the exertion. He carries an umbrella and strolls front.)*

STAGE MANAGER. *(front)* Well! There are some *living* people. There's Joe Stoddard, our undertaker, supervising a new-made grave. And here comes a Grover's Corners boy, that left town to go out West.

SAM CRAIG. Good afternoon, Joe Stoddard.

JOE STODDARD. *(turns, surprised)* Good afternoon, good afternoon. Let me see now: do I know you?

SAM CRAIG. I'm Sam Craig.

JOE STODDARD. Gracious sakes' alive! Of all people! I should'a knowed you'd be back for the funeral. You've been away a long time, Sam.

SAM CRAIG. Yes, I've been away over twelve years. I'm in business out in Buffalo now, Joe. But I was in the East when I got news of my cousin's death, so I thought I'd combine things a little and come and see the old home. You look well.

JOE STODDARD. Yes, yes, can't complain. Very sad, our journey today, Samuel.

SAM CRAIG. Yes.

JOE STODDARD. Yes, yes. I always say I hate to supervise when a young person is taken.

(SAM turns, glancing at the gravestones, crossing to Farmer McCarty. JOE looks off left.)

They'll be here in a few minutes now. I had to come here early today – my son's supervisin' at the home.

SAM CRAIG. *(reading stones)* Old Farmer McCarty, I used to do chores for him – after school. He had the lumbago.

JOE STODDARD. Yes, we brought Farmer McCarty here a number of years ago now.

SAM CRAIG. *(staring at MRS. GIBBS' knees)* Why, this is my Aunt Julia...I'd forgotten that she'd...of course, of course.

JOE STODDARD. Yes, Doc Gibbs lost his wife two-three years ago...about this time. And today's another pretty bad blow for him, too.

MRS. GIBBS. *(to SIMON STIMSON: in an even voice)* That's my sister Carey's boy, Sam...Sam Craig.

SIMON STIMSON. I'm always uncomfortable when *they're* around.

MRS. GIBBS. Simon.

SAM CRAIG. Do they choose their own verses much, Joe?

JOE STODDARD. No...not usual. Mostly the bereaved pick a verse.

SAM CRAIG. Doesn't sound like Aunt Julia. There aren't many of those Hersey sisters left now. Let me see: where are...I wanted to look at my father's and mother's...

(His eyes fall on Stimson's stone.)

JOE STODDARD. Over there with the Craigs...Avenue F.

SAM CRAIG. *(reading Simon Stimson's epitaph.)* He was organist at church, wasn't he? – Hm, drank a lot, we used to say.

JOE STODDARD. Nobody was supposed to know about it. He'd seen a peck of trouble. *(behind his hand)* Took his own life, y' know?

SAM CRAIG. Oh, did he?

JOE STODDARD. Hung himself in the attic. They tried to hush it up, but of course it got around. He chose his own epy-taph. You can see it there. It ain't a verse exactly.

SAM CRAIG. Why, it's just some notes of music – what is it?

JOE STODDARD. Oh, I wouldn't know. It was wrote up in the Boston papers at the time.

SAM CRAIG. Joe, what did she die of?

JOE STODDARD. Who?

SAM CRAIG. My cousin.

JOE STODDARD. Oh, didn't you know? Had some trouble bringing a baby into the world. 'Twas her second, though. There's a little boy 'bout four years old.

SAM CRAIG. *(opening his umbrella)* The grave's going to be over there?

JOE STODDARD. Yes, there ain't much more room over here among the Gibbses, so they're opening up a whole new Gibbs section over by Avenue B. You'll excuse me now. I see they're comin'.

(From left to center, at the back of the stage, comes a procession. **FOUR MEN** *carry a casket, invisible to us. All the rest are under umbrellas. One can vaguely see:* **DR. GIBBS, GEORGE,** *the* **WEBBS,** *etc. They gather about a grave in the back center of the stage, a little to the left of center.* **EMILY** *is among them, a black cloak covering her white dress.)*

MRS. SOAMES. Who is it, Julia?

MRS. GIBBS. *(without raising her eyes)* My daughter-in-law, Emily Webb.

MRS. SOAMES. *(a little surprised, but no emotion)* Well, I declare! The road up here must have been awful muddy. What did she die of, Julia?

MRS. GIBBS. In childbirth.

MRS. SOAMES. Childbirth. *(almost with a laugh)* I'd forgotten all about that. My, wasn't life awful – *(with a sigh)* and wonderful.

SIMON STIMSON. *(with a sideways glance)* Wonderful, was it?

MRS. GIBBS. Simon! Now, remember!

MRS. SOAMES. I remember Emily's wedding. Wasn't it a lovely wedding! And I remember her reading the class poem at Graduation Exercises. Emily was one of the brightest girls ever graduated from High School. I've heard Principal Wilkins say so time after time. I called on them at their new farm, just before I died. Perfectly beautiful farm.

A WOMAN FROM AMONG THE DEAD. It's on the same road we lived on.

A MAN AMONG THE DEAD. Yepp, right smart farm.

(They subside. The **FUNERAL GROUP** *by the grave starts singing "Blessed Be the Tie That Binds".)*

A WOMAN AMONG THE DEAD. I always liked that hymn. I was hopin' they'd sing a hymn.

(Pause. Suddenly **EMILY** *appears from among the umbrellas. She is wearing a white dress. Her hair is down her back and tied by a white ribbon like a little girl. She comes slowly, gazing wonderingly at the dead, a little dazed.)*

(She stops halfway and smiles faintly. After looking at the mourners for a moment, she walks slowly to the vacant chair beside **MRS. GIBBS** *and sits down.)*

EMILY. *(to them all, quietly, smiling)* Hello.

MRS. SOAMES. Hello, Emily.

A MAN AMONG THE DEAD. Hello, M's Gibbs.

EMILY. *(warmly)* Hello, Mother Gibbs.

MRS. GIBBS. Emily.

EMILY. Hello. *(with surprise)* It's raining. *(Her eyes drift back to the funeral company.)*

MRS. GIBBS. Yes…They'll be gone soon, dear. Just rest yourself.

EMILY. It seems thousands and thousands of years since I… *(The* **FUNERAL GROUP** *sings second verse of "Blest Be the Tie That Binds".)* Papa remembered that that was my favorite hymn. Oh, I wish I'd been here a long time. I don't like being new here. – How do you do, Mr. Stimson?

SIMON STIMSON. *(firmly)* How do you do, Emily.

*(***EMILY** *continues to look about her with a wondering smile; as though to shut out from her mind the thought of the funeral company she starts speaking to* **MRS. GIBBS** *with a touch of nervousness.)*

EMILY. Mother Gibbs, George and I have made that farm into just the best place you ever saw. We thought of you all the time. We wanted to show you the new barn and a great long ce-ment drinking fountain for the stock. We bought that out of the money you left us.

MRS. GIBBS. I did?

EMILY. Don't you remember, Mother Gibbs – the legacy you left us? Why, it was over three hundred and fifty dollars.

(The **FUNERAL GROUP** *breaks up and begins to exit slowly. A* **SMALL GROUP** *only remains at grave:* **MR.** *and* **MRS. WEBB,** **GEORGE** *and* **DR. GIBBS,** *who has no umbrella.)*

MRS. GIBBS. Yes, yes, Emily.

EMILY. Well, there's a patent device on the drinking fountain so that it never overflows, Mother Gibbs, and it never sinks below a certain mark they have there. It's fine. *(Her voice trails off and her eyes return to the funeral.)* It won't be the same to George without me, but it's a lovely farm.

*(Suddenly she looks directly at **MRS. GIBBS**.)*

Live people don't understand, do they?

MRS. GIBBS. No, dear – not very much.

EMILY. They're sort of shut up in little boxes, aren't they? I feel as though I knew them last a thousand years ago... My boy is spending the day at Mrs. Carter's.

*(She sees **MR. CARTER** among the dead.)*

Oh, Mr. Carter, my little boy is spending the day at your house.

MR. CARTER. Is he?

EMILY. Yes, he loves it there. – Mother Gibbs, we have a Ford, too. Never gives any trouble. I don't drive, though. *(pause)* Mother Gibbs, when does this feeling go away? – Of being...one of *them?* How long does it...?

MRS. GIBBS. Sh! dear. Just wait and be patient.

*(**MR.** and **MRS. WEBB** and **GEORGE** slowly exit.)*

EMILY. *(with a sigh)* I know. – Look, they're finished. They're going.

MRS. GIBBS. Sh – .

*(**DR. GIBBS** kneels to take flowers from grave, slowly rises and comes over to his wife's grave and stands before it a moment. **EMILY** looks up at his face. **MRS. GIBBS** does not raise her eyes.)*

EMILY. Look! Father Gibbs is bringing some of my flowers to you. He looks just like George, doesn't he?

*(***DR. GIBBS*** *lays flowers at his wife's feet, head bowed and sighs.)*

Oh, Mother Gibbs, I never realized before how troubled and how...how in the dark live persons are. Look at him. I loved him so. *(long pause)*

*(***DR. GIBBS*** *exits slowly, putting his hat on when he is nearly off.)*

From morning till night, that's all they are – troubled.

THE DEAD. Little cooler than it was. – Yes, that rain's cooled it off a little. Those northeast winds always do the same thing, don't they? If it isn't a rain, it's a three-day blow. –

*(A patient calm falls on the stage. The ***STAGE MANAGER*** appears at his proscenium pillar, smoking.* ***EMILY*** *sits up abruptly with an idea.)*

EMILY. But, Mother Gibbs, one can go back; one can go back there again...into living. I feel it. I know it. Why just then for a moment I was thinking about...about the farm...and for a minute I *was* there, and my baby was on my lap as plain as day.

MRS. GIBBS. Yes, of course you can.

EMILY. *(excited)* I can go back there and live all those days over again...why not?

MRS. GIBBS. All I can say is, Emily, don't.

EMILY. *(She appeals urgently to the* ***STAGE MANAGER.****)* But it's true, isn't it? I can go and live...back there... again.

STAGE MANAGER. *(quietly)* Yes, some have tried – but they soon come back here.

MRS. GIBBS. *(gently)* Don't do it, Emily.

MRS. SOAMES. Emily, don't. It's not what you think it'd be.

EMILY. *(eagerly)* But I won't live over a sad day. I'll choose a happy one – I'll choose the day I first knew that I loved George. Why should that be painful?

(They are silent. Her question turns to the **STAGE MANAGER.** *)*

STAGE MANAGER. You not only live it; but you watch yourself living it.

EMILY. Yes?

STAGE MANAGER. And as you watch it, you see the thing that they – down there – never know. You see the future. You know what's going to happen afterwards.

EMILY. But is that – painful? Why?

MRS. GIBBS. That's not the only reason why you shouldn't do it, Emily. When you've been here longer you'll see that our life here is to forget all that, and think only of what's ahead, and be ready for what's ahead. When you've been here longer you'll understand.

EMILY. *(softly)* But, Mother Gibbs, how can I *ever* forget that life? It's all I know. It's all I had.

MRS. SOAMES. Oh, Emily. It isn't wise. Really, it isn't.

EMILY. But it's a thing I must know for myself. I'll choose a happy day, anyway.

MRS. GIBBS. *No!* – At least, choose an unimportant day. Choose the least important day in your life. It will be important enough.

EMILY. *(to herself:)* Then it can't be since I was married; or since the baby was born. *(to the* **STAGE MANAGER,** *eagerly:)* I can choose a birthday at least, can't I? – I choose my twelfth birthday.

STAGE MANAGER. All right. February 11th, 1899. A Tuesday. – Do you want any special time of day?

EMILY. Oh, I want the whole day.

STAGE MANAGER. We'll begin at dawn. You remember it had been snowing for several days; but it had stopped the night before, and they had begun clearing the roads. The sun's coming up.

(The stage at no time in this act has been very dark; but now the left half of the stage gradually becomes very bright – the brightness of a crisp winter morning.)

EMILY. *(with a cry; rising)* There's Main Street...why, that's Mr. Morgan's drugstore before he changed it!...And there's the livery stable.

*(***EMILY*** walks toward Main Street.)*

STAGE MANAGER. Yes, it's 1899. This is fourteen years ago.

EMILY. Oh, that's the town I knew as a little girl. And, *look,* there's the old white fence that used to be around our house. Oh, I'd forgotten that! Oh, I love it so! *(She turns eagerly to the* **STAGE MANAGER.** *)* Are they inside?

STAGE MANAGER. Yes, your mother'll be coming downstairs in a minute to make breakfast.

EMILY. *(softly)* Will she?

STAGE MANAGER. And you remember: your father had been away for several days; he came back on the early-morning train.

EMILY. No...?

STAGE MANAGER. He'd been back to his college to make a speech – in western New York, at Clinton.

EMILY. Look! There's Howie Newsome. There's our policeman. *(looks at* **STAGE MANAGER,** *confused)* But he's *dead;* he *died.*

(The voices of **HOWIE NEWSOME, CONSTABLE WARREN** *and* **JOE CROWELL, JR.,** *are heard at the left of the stage.* **EMILY** *listens in delight.)*

HOWIE NEWSOME. Whoa, Bessie! – Bessie! 'Morning, Bill.

CONSTABLE WARREN. Morning, Howie.

HOWIE NEWSOME. You're up early.

CONSTABLE WARREN. Been rescuin' a party; darn near froze to death, down by Polish Town thar. Got drunk and lay out in the snowdrifts. Thought he was in bed when I shook'm.

EMILY. Why, there's Joe Crowell....

JOE CROWELL. Good morning, Mr. Warren. 'Morning, Howie.

(MRS. WEBB has appeared in her kitchen, but EMILY does not see her until she calls.)

MRS. WEBB. Chil-*dren!* Wally! Emily!...Time to get up. *(turns to stove and quickly adds coal to fire)*

EMILY. *(has turned excitedly on hearing her mother's voice, and now hurries behind her)* Mama, I'm here! Oh! how young Mama looks! I didn't know Mama was ever that young.

(HOWIE NEWSOME has entered along Main Street to the sound of milk bottles and brings the milk to MRS. WEBB's door.)

MRS. WEBB. *(calling upstairs)* You can come and dress by the kitchen fire, if you like; but hurry. *(hurries to meet HOWIE)* Good morning, Mr. Newsome. Whhhh – it's cold.

HOWIE NEWSOME. Ten below by my barn, Mrs. Webb. *(handing her two bottles of milk)*

(HOWIE exits.)

MRS. WEBB. Think of it! Keep yourself wrapped up.

(She picks up album and takes her bottles in, shuddering.)

(From this point on, she moves no more than two short steps from stove, suggesting movements about the kitchen, rather than pacing them.)

EMILY. *(with an effort)* Mama, I can't find my blue hair ribbon anywhere.

(**CONSTABLE WARREN** *slowly enters.*)

MRS. WEBB. *(turning at stove to call upstairs)* Just open your eyes, dear, that's all. I laid it out for you special – on the dresser, there. If it were a snake it would bite you. *(turns to start breakfast at stove, her moves more confined and less realistic than in previous acts)*

(**MR. WEBB** *slowly enters.*)

EMILY. Yes, yes... *(smiling agreement as mother reacts as she hoped)*

(**EMILY** *puts her hand on her heart.* **MR. WEBB** *comes along Main Street to center, where he meets* **CONSTABLE WARREN**. *Their movements and voices are increasingly lively in the sharp air.*)

(**MRS. WEBB** *crosses to cupboard for dishes and silver, then to set table where it used to stand, making two quick trips.*)

MR. WEBB. Good morning, Bill.

CONSTABLE WARREN. Good morning, Mr. Webb. You're up early.

(**EMILY**, *ecstatic at seeing her father, watches him as he enters, never taking her eyes off of him.*)

MR. WEBB. Yes, just been back to my old college in New York State. Been any trouble here?

CONSTABLE WARREN. Well, I was called up this mornin' to rescue a Polish fella – darn near froze to death he was.

MR. WEBB. We must get it in the paper.

(**MRS. WEBB** *crosses to putter at stove.*)

CONSTABLE WARREN. 'Twan't much.

EMILY. *(whispers)* Papa.

(**MR. WEBB** *shakes the snow off his feet and enters his house.* **CONSTABLE WARREN** *goes off, right.*)

MR. WEBB. Good morning, Mother. *(removes his hat and coat)*

MRS. WEBB. How did it go, Charles?

MR. WEBB. Oh, fine, I guess. I told'm a few things. – Everything all right here?

MRS. WEBB. Yes – can't think of anything that's happened, special. Been right cold. Howie Newsome says it's ten below over to his barn.

MR. WEBB. Yes, well, it's colder than that at Hamilton College. Students' ears are falling off. It ain't Christian. – Paper have any mistakes in it?

MRS. WEBB. None that I noticed. Coffee's ready when you want it. *(He starts upstairs.)* Charles! Don't forget, it's Emily's birthday. Did you remember to get her something?

MR. WEBB. *(patting his pocket)* Yes, I've got something here. *(calling up the stairs)* Where's my girl? Where's my birthday girl?

(He goes off left.)

MRS. WEBB. Don't interrupt her now, Charles. You can see her at breakfast. She's slow enough as it is. Hurry up, children! It's seven o'clock. Now, I don't want to call you again. *(She turns to pare potatoes at table near stove.)*

EMILY. *(softly, more in wonder than in grief)* I can't bear it. They're so young and beautiful. Why did they ever have to get old? Mama, I'm here. I'm grown up. I love you all, everything. – I can't look at everything hard enough.

*(She looks questioningly at the **STAGE MANAGER**, saying or suggesting: "Can I go in?" He nods briefly. She crosses to the inner door to the kitchen, left of her mother, and as though entering the room, says, suggesting the voice of a girl of twelve:)*

EMILY. Good morning, Mama.

MRS. WEBB. *(crossing to embrace and kiss her; in her characteristic matter-of-fact manner)* Well, now, dear, a very happy birthday to my girl and many happy returns. *(She returns to the stove, slipping out of* **EMILY**'s *arms which were about to embrace her.)* There are some surprises waiting for you on the kitchen table.

EMILY. Oh, Mama, you *shouldn't* have. *(She throws an anguished glance at the* **STAGE MANAGER**.) I can't – I can't.

MRS. WEBB. *(facing the audience, over her stove)* But birthday or no birthday, I want you to eat your breakfast good and slow. I want you to grow up and be a good strong girl.

*(***EMILY** *steps to table and looks over gifts.)*

That in the blue paper is from your Aunt Carrie; and I reckon you can guess who brought the post-card album. I found it on the doorstep when I brought in the milk – George Gibbs...must have come over in the cold pretty early...right nice of him. *(putters at stove again)*

EMILY. *(To herself. Very gently picking up album.)* Oh, George! I'd forgotten that....

MRS. WEBB. Chew that bacon good and slow. It'll help keep you warm on a cold day.

EMILY. *(with mounting urgency)* Oh, Mama, just look at me one minute as though you really saw me.

*(***MRS. WEBB** *turns to stir oatmeal at stove, placid and smiling, not hearing.)*

Mama, fourteen years have gone by. I'm dead. You're a grandmother, Mama. I married George Gibbs, Mama. Wally's dead, too. Mama, his appendix burst on a camping trip to North Conway. We felt just terrible about it – don't you remember? But, just for a moment now we're all together. Mama, just for a moment we're happy. *Let's look at one another.*

MRS. WEBB. *(puts dish on table)* That in the yellow paper is something I found in the attic among your grandmother's things. You're old enough to wear it now, and I thought you'd like it.

EMILY. And this is from you. Why, Mama, it's just lovely and it's just what I wanted. It's beautiful!

(She flings her arms around her mother's neck. Her **MOTHER** *goes on with her cooking, but is pleased.)*

MRS. WEBB. Well, I hoped you'd like it. Hunted all over. Your Aunt Norah couldn't find one in Concord, so I had to send all the way to Boston. *(laughing)* Wally has something for you, too. He made it at manual-training class and he's very proud of it. Be sure you make a big fuss about it. – Your father has a surprise for you, too; don't know what it is myself. Sh – here he comes.

MR. WEBB. *(offstage)* Where's my girl? Where's my birthday girl?

EMILY. *(in a loud voice to the* **STAGE MANAGER***)* I can't. I can't go on. It goes so fast. We don't have time to look at one another. *(She breaks down sobbing.)*

(The lights dim on the left half of the stage. **MRS. WEBB** *disappears.)*

I didn't realize. So all that was going on and we never noticed. Take me back – up the hill – to my grave. But first: Wait! One more look. Good-by, Good-by, world. Good-by, Grover's Corners... Mama and Papa. Good-by to clocks ticking...and Mama's sunflowers. And food and coffee. And new-ironed dresses and hot baths...and sleeping and waking up. Oh, earth, you're too wonderful for anybody to realize you. *(She looks toward the* **STAGE MANAGER** *and asks abruptly, through her tears:)* Do any human beings ever realize life while they live it? – every, every minute?

STAGE MANAGER. No. *(pause)* The saints and poets, maybe – they do some.

EMILY. *(calmly, as she absorbs the thought)* I'm ready to go back.

(She returns to her chair beside **MRS. GIBBS**. *As she does so the lights dim, leaving only a deep blue except for amber on the Dead.)*

(pause)

MRS. GIBBS. Were you happy?

EMILY. No…I should have listened to you. That's all human beings are! Just blind people.

MRS. GIBBS. Look, it's clearing up. The stars are coming out.

EMILY. Oh, Mr. Stimson, I should have listened to them.

SIMON STIMSON. *(with mounting violence; bitingly)* Yes, now you know. Now you know! That's what it was to be alive. To move about in a cloud of ignorance; to go up and down trampling on the feelings of those…of those about you. To spend and waste time as though you had a million years. To be always at the mercy of one self-centered passion, or another. Now you know – that's the happy existence you wanted to go back to. Ignorance and blindness.

MRS. GIBBS. *(spiritedly)* Simon Stimson, that ain't the whole truth and you know it. Emily, look at that star. I forget its name.

A MAN AMONG THE DEAD. My boy Joel was a sailor, – knew 'em all. He'd set on the porch evenings and tell 'em all by name. Yes, sir, wonderful!

ANOTHER MAN AMONG THE DEAD. A star's mighty good company.

A WOMAN AMONG THE DEAD. Yes. Yes, 'tis.

SIMON STIMSON. Here's one of *them* coming.

THE DEAD. That's funny. 'Tain't no time for one of them to be here. – Goodness sakes.

EMILY. Mother Gibbs, it's George.

MRS. GIBBS. Sh, dear. Just rest yourself.

EMILY. It's George.

(GEORGE enters, hat in hand, and slowly comes toward them.)

A MAN FROM AMONG THE DEAD. And my boy, Joel, who knew the stars – he used to say it took millions of years for that speck o' light to git to the earth. Don't seem like a body could believe it, but that's what he used to say – millions of years.

(GEORGE sinks to his knees then falls full length at EMILY's feet.)

A WOMAN AMONG THE DEAD. Goodness! That ain't no way to behave!

MRS. SOAMES. He ought to be home.

EMILY. Mother Gibbs?

MRS. GIBBS. Yes, Emily?

EMILY. They don't understand, do they?

MRS. GIBBS. No, dear. They don't understand.

(train whistle offstage)

(The STAGE MANAGER appears at the right, one hand on a dark curtain which he slowly draws across the scene.)

(In the distance a clock is heard striking the hour very faintly.)

STAGE MANAGER. Most everybody's asleep in Grover's Corners. There are a few lights on: Shorty Hawkins, down at the depot, has just watched the Albany train go by. And at the livery stable somebody's setting up late and talking. – Yes, it's clearing up. There are the stars – doing their old, old crisscross journeys in the sky. Scholars haven't settled the matter yet, but they seem to think there are no living beings up there. Just chalk...or fire. Only this one is straining away, straining away all the time to make something of itself. The strain's so bad that every sixteen hours everybody lies down and gets a rest. *(He winds his watch.)* Hm...Eleven o'clock in Grover's Corners. – You get a good rest, too. Good night.

The End

NOTE ON PANTOMIME

While it is impossible in the script to describe in complete detail the many moments of pantomime, some indications may be of service in reproducing it:

MRS. GIBBS' BREAKFAST starts by raising the window shade, putting up window with both hands, turning to stove, lifting off lids with a handle-holder, putting holder down, placing kindling in stove from box beside it, taking match from box above stove, scratching it on box, lighting fire, replacing stove lids, etc.

MR. MORGAN'S MIXING OF SODAS starts with him taking two glasses from higher shelf and placing them on lower. He takes syrup bottle, removes stopper, pours into both glasses, replaces stopper and bottle. Takes one glass, turns right, removes lid from ice-cream receptacle, takes ice cream scoop and puts cream into glass. Repeats with second glass, replaces lid of receptacle. Holds first glass up to soda faucet and turns old-fashioned wheel faucet. Sets glass down and repeats with second.

All pantomime should be worked out realistically and in at least sufficient detail so that the actor definitely knows what he is doing. If, however, the pantomime is too detailed, it will distract from the lines of the Stage Manager or even from the actors who are pantomiming. A happy medium should be struck between pantomime which tells its own story and definitely underdone miming. In other words, it should be kept as a background effect.

NOTE ON WEDDING ENTRANCE

This can be one of the most effective movements in the play if properly handled. It should not be realistic, but merely a dignified entrance of actors getting into place.

The **CONGREGATION** should gather as near as possible to the Right and Left tormentors, lined up to follow each other as they are to sit in the "pews". On the sixth stroke of the chimes (as the dim "wall lights" come up on their faces) the two people who are to sit in central-aisle seats of the second rows from the pulpit start slowly walking to the outer end of their "pews" and into place to sit. When they have progressed some five feet from the start, the persons leading the first (or family) and third lines start. When third-line leaders have progressed some five feet, those leading the fourth line start. In each case the leaders are followed at about three-foot distances by others in their "pews". This arrangement produces a wedge-like formation from either side, which, as the church lights gradually form (per light plot), is tremendously effective from the front.

By no means all the seats in the church need be filled. The congregation should remain unmoved, merely pictorial, except for two moments: (1)when the wedding-march starts they should move expectantly and gradually turn to watch the **BRIDE** pass up the aisle, and (2)as the **COUPLE** go down the aisle they should rise, chatting, and watch the **COUPLE** throughout the exit.

Blessed Be the Tie That Binds

(Orig. key – F maj.)

Bless'd be — the tie — that binds Our hearts — in Chris — tian love; The
fel — low – ship — of kin — dred minds – is like — to that — a — bove.

Before our Father's throne
We pour our ardent prayers;
Our fears, our hopes, our aims are one
Our comforts and our cares.

We share each other's woes,
Our mutual burdens bear;
And often for each other flows
The sympathizing tear.

Additional Verses:

When we asunder part,
It gives us inward pain;
But we shall still be joined in heart,
And hope to meet again.

This glorious hope revives
Our courage by the way;
While each in expectation lives,
And longs to see the day.

From sorrow, toil and pain,
And sin, we shall be free,
And perfect love and friendship reign
Through all eternity

Art Thou Weary, Art Thou Languid

(Orig. key – G maj

Art thou wea – ry, Art thou lan – guid, Are thou sore dis — trest?
Hath He marks to lead me to Him, If He be my guide?

"Come to —— me" saith One, "And — com – ing be at rest."
"In His —— feet and hands are — woundprints and His side."

Love Divine All Loves Excelling

(Orig. key – B♭ maj.

Love di – vine, All loves ex — celling, Joy of heav'n —— to earth come – down.

Fix in us Thy hum-ble — dwel - ling All Thy faith - ful mer - cies — crown.
Vis – it us with Thy sal — va — tion En – ter ev' – ry trembl – ing — heart.

Je – sus Thou art All com — pas – sion Pure un - bound - ed love Thou – art.

Breathe, oh, breathe thy loving spirit
Into every troubled breast;
Let us all in three inherit;
Let us find thy promised rest.
Take away the love of sinning;
Alpha and Omega be;
End of faith, as its beginning,
Set our hearts at liberty.

PROPERTY PLOT

A NOTE ON PROPERTIES

The use of many props is indicated in this script, but except for those used by the **STAGE MANAGER, MR. WEBB'S** handkerchief used as a bandage in Act I, and the umbrellas used in Act III, it must be understood that all are imagined.

OFFSTAGE LEFT:

16 assorted rehearsal chairs

1 trellis, portable, with roses

20 wet umbrellas

1 cane (**CONSTABLE WARREN**)

1 table about 21" x 36"

1 box about 11" x 20" x 14" for pulpit

1 wooden piano bench

1 stepladder, black, on wheels

1 handkerchief for bandage (**MR. WEBB**)

OFFSTAGE RIGHT:

16 assorted rehearsal chairs (2 with straight backs to be used left of table center stageright for board in soda fountain scene; 1 with short legs for **WALLY** in Act III)

1 table about 2' square

1 prompt Mss (**STAGE MANAGER**)

1 pipe (**STAGE MANAGER**)

1 pocket watch (**STAGE MANAGER**)

2 stools (soda fountain)

1 dry umbrella (**SAM CRAIG**)

1 organ

1 baseball bat (**1ST BASEBALL PLAYER**)

1 baseball glove (**2ND BASEBALL PLAYER**)

1 eight-foot board (soda fountain scene)

1 stepladder wide enough for **GEORGE** and **REBECCA**, on wheels, black

1 trellis with vines

SOUND EFFECTS:

Train whistle

Factory whistle

Schoolbell

Milk bottles (bottles in rack off)

Cockcrow (vocal)

Crickets (vocal)

Whinny (vocal)

Chickens (vocal)

Thunder (drum)

Church Chimes (pipes, C sharp and D)

Town clock (use same)

Newspapers (newspapers wrapped and skidded on floor)

THE ORCHESTRA PIT:

1 portable organ

2 benches to hold 5 people each

1 box for Stimson to stand on

COSTUME PLOT

In the original production the costumes were designed for the 1901-1904 period without emphasis on what might prove the amusing element.

STAGE MANAGER

Worn gray suit. Old tan shoes. Gray felt hat. Coat worn open. Vest unbuttoned two top buttons. Spectacles for "**MR. MORGAN.**"

MRS. GIBBS

Act I. Dark blue woolen dress. Blue striped waist. Flowered apron. For return from choir meeting, same with hat and lace collar. Low black shoes and gray cotton stockings throughout. Blond pompadour wig.

Act II. Same, with gray knitted shawl. For wedding: add dark blue sailor hat and gray lace collar, and dark blue tippet.

Act III. Same as Act I minus apron.

MRS. WEBB

Act I. Dark gray woolen skirt. Brown cotton waist. Blue checked kitchen apron. For return from choir practice, remove apron and add brown hat and lace collar.

Act II. Same for first scene as at opening of Act I. For wedding add hat and green shoulder cape.

Act III. For funeral, black cape, hat and mourning veil. For later scene, blue sweater and apron over previous skirt and waist. Black shoes and gray cotton stockings throughout.

EMILY

Act I. Blue woolen jumper skirt. Light blue middy waist and black tie. Black hair bow. Gray woolen stockings and Mary Jane slippers.

Act II. Flowered cotton print dress. Same bow and shoes, with white stockings. For wedding: white wedding dress and veil, with stiff muslin petticoat. White shoes.

Act III. Same as for wedding minus veil, substituting limp cotton petticoat. Black floor-length cape for funeral entrance (given to an extra as she leaves group.)

MRS. SOAMES

Act I. Blue woolen skirt. Green plaid waist. Blue straw hat. Black Oxfords and gray stockings.

Act II. Same with jabot added.

Act III. Same as Act I minus hat.

DR. GIBBS

Acts I and II. Brown, loose-fitting, 3-button suit. Brown shoes and socks. Leghorn hat.

Act III. Dark overcoat and gray felt hat. Throughout: white shirt, low turnover collar, black string tie.

MR. WEBB

Act I. Gray tweed suit. Light gray checked vest. Blue shirt with white turnover collar. Black bow tie. Handkerchief held around right middle finger as bandage. Armbands to show when mowing lawn. Final scene in act; gray soft hat.

Act II: Same trousers. Black sack coat and vest.

Act III: Black topcoat for funeral. For final scene: black ulster and gray hat over full black suit.

GEORGE

Act I. Tight gray checked woolen trousers. Peppermint striped shirt with high turnover collar and cuffs. Red bow tie. Black shoes.

Act II. Dark blue trousers. Brown sweater. Brown striped turtle-necked dicky to permit underdressing of white shirt. For wedding: same trousers with 4-button coat to match. White shirt and high turnover collar. Black tie (four-in-hand).

Act III: Long black overcoat over wedding suit. Carry soft brown hat.

HOWIE NEWSOME

Act I. Blue overalls over old brown trousers. Heavy working shoes throughout play. Gray workshirt and gray sweater. Woolen cap (earmuff type).

Act II. Same. For Wedding: tweed gray-brown suit. White shirt and collar. String tie. Brown felt hat.

Act III. For funeral: long black coat and gray trousers, brown felt hat. For final scene: overalls with mackinaw. Same cap with earmuffs down. Mittens.

REBECCA

Act I. Blue checked gingham dress. Brown stockings. Black slippers. Blue hair-ribbon.

Act II: (wedding). Tan and blue checked dress. Blue hair ribbon.

JOE CROWELL

Gray knickers. Brown sweater. Pink shirt. Brown shoes and long brown stockings.

PROF. WILLARD

Dark blue serge, shiny, double-breasted suit, coat unbuttoned. Black shoes. White collar and shirt. Black bow tie. Gold spectacles.

WOMAN IN BOX

Black street ensemble. Ponyskin cape. Gardenias. Black tricorner hat.

MAN IN AUDITORIUM

Dark business suit.

CONSTABLE WARREN

Throughout: Loose black suit. Black shoes. White shirt and collar. Dark tie. Gray felt hat worn flat. Spectacles.

SIMON STIMSON

Gray suit and tie. White shirt and high standing collar. Black shoes.

SI CROWELL

Long brown woolen pants. Brown sweater. Brown checked shirt open at neck. Brown shoes and gray socks.

SAM CRAIG

Black suit. Black silk socks. Black shoes. White shirt and turnover collar. Blue tie. Derby hat.

JOE STODDARD

Gray Prince Albert. White shirt and turnover collar. Black bow tie. Black shoes and socks. Black felt hat.

WALLY

Act I. Dark blue serge knickers. Blue shirt and blue bow tie. Black shoes and long black stockings.

Act III. Same, with blue serge coat.

1ST BALLPLAYER

Old gray trousers. Blouse of gray baseball uniform. Black sneakers. Baseball glove.

2ND BALLPLAYER

Blue overalls. White torn shirt. Black sweater around shoulders. Black sneakers. Baseball bat.

3RD BALLPLAYER

Brown trousers. Brown sweater. White shirt. Black sneakers. Baseball cap.

1ST MAN FROM AMONG THE DEAD

Black Prince Albert. Standing collar. Black bow tie. Black shoes. Moustache.

2ND MAN FROM AMONG THE DEAD

Black Prince Albert. Standing high solar. Black four-in-hand tie. Beard.

1ST WOMAN FROM AMONG THE DEAD

Dark brown skirt. Figured brown waist. Black shoes and stockings.

2ND WOMAN FROM AMONG THE DEAD

Brown tweed skirt. Green waist. Black shoes and stockings.

FARMER MCCARTY

Black Prince Albert. Black shoes, stockings, four-in-hand tie. Wing collar.

EXTRAS

Men in dark colors throughout. Carry hats in wedding and funeral both. Women's skirts dark throughout. Waists colored for wedding, covered by dark capes and coats for funeral. Men wear dark coats for funeral.

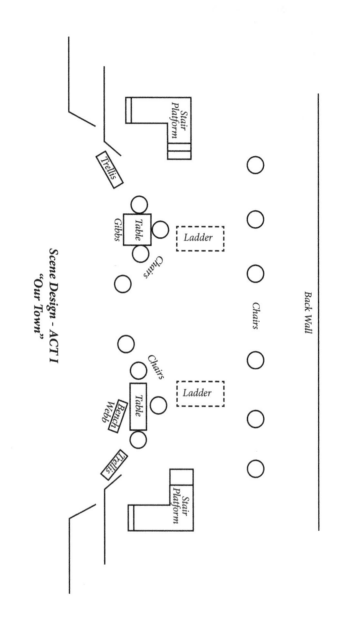

Scene Design - ACT I
"Our Town"

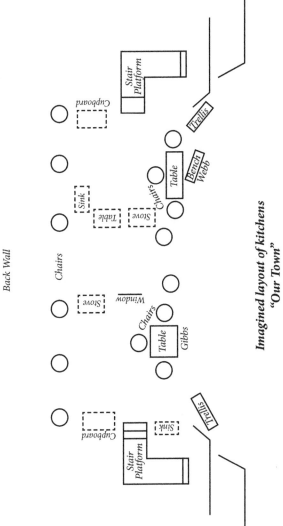

Imagined layout of kitchens
"Our Town"

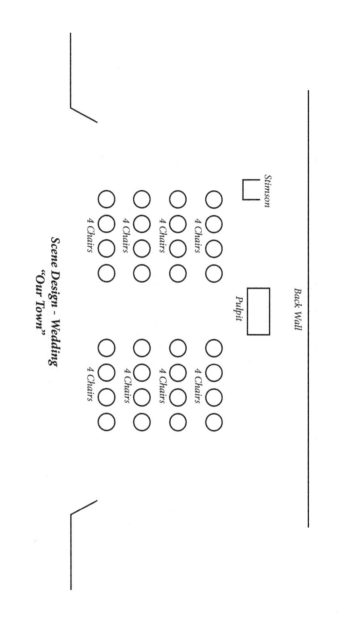

Back Wall

Stimson

Pulpit

4 Chairs
4 Chairs
4 Chairs
4 Chairs

4 Chairs
4 Chairs
4 Chairs
4 Chairs

Scene Design - Wedding
"Our Town"

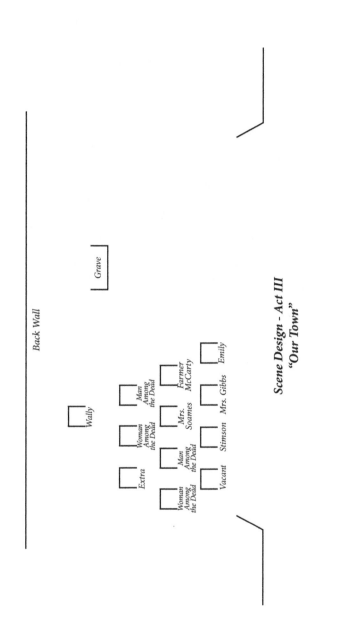

Scene Design - Act III
"Our Town"

ABOUT THORNTON WILDER

Born in Madison, Wisconsin, and educated at Yale and Princeton, Thornton Wilder (1897-1975) was an accomplished novelist and playwright whose works explore the connection between the commonplace and the cosmic dimensions of human experience. *The Bridge of San Luis Rey*, one of his seven novels, won the Pulitzer Prize in 1928, and his next-to-last novel, *The Eighth Day* received the National Book Award (1968). Two of his four major plays garnered Pulitzer Prizes, *Our Town* (1938) and *The Skin of Our Teeth* (1943). His play, *The Matchmaker* ran on Broadway for 486 performances (1955-1957), Wilder's Broadway record, and was later adapted into the musical *Hello, Dolly!* Wilder also enjoyed enormous success with many other forms of the written and spoken word, among them translation, acting, opera librettos, lecturing, teaching and film (his screenplay for Alfred Hitchcock's 1943 psycho-thriller, *Shadow of a Doubt* remains a classic to this day). Letter writing held a central place in Wilder's life, and since his death, three volumes of his letters have been published. Wilder's many honors include the Gold Medal for Fiction from the American Academy of Arts and Letters, the Presidential Medal of Freedom, and the National Book Committee's Medal for Literature. On April 17, 1997, the centenary of his birth, the US Postal Service unveiled the Thornton Wilder 32-cent stamp in Hamden, Connecticut, his official address after 1930 and where he died on December 7, 1975.

For more information, visit www.thorntonwilder.com.

Also by
Thornton Wilder...

The Alcestiad
The Beaux' Stratagem (with Ken Ludwig)
The Matchmaker
The Skin of Our Teeth

<u>**Thornton Wilder One Act Series: The Ages of Man**</u>
Infancy
Childhood
Youth
Rivers Under the Earth

<u>**Thornton Wilder One Act Series: The Seven Deadly Sins**</u>
The Drunken Sisters
Bernice
The Wreck on the 5:25
A Ringing of Doorbells
In Shakespeare and the Bible
Someone From Assisi
Cement Hands

<u>**Thornton Wilder One Act Series: Wilder's Classic One Acts**</u>
The Long Christmas Dinner
Queens of France
Pullman Car Hiawatha
Love and How to Cure It
Such Things Only Happen in Books
The Happy Journey to Trenton and Camden

Please visit our website **samuelfrench.com** for complete
descriptions and licensing information.